SINGAPORE

Books by John Ball

SINGAPORE

A Virgil Tibbs Mystery Novel

John Ball

Dodd, Mead & Company
New York

Copyright © 1986 by John Ball

Published by Dodd, Mead & Company, Inc.
79 Madison Avenue, New York, N.Y. 10016
Distributed in Canada by
McClelland and Stewart Limited, Toronto
Manufactured in the United States of America
Designed by Erich Hobbing

First Edition

Library of Congress Cataloging in Publication Data

Ball, John Dudley, 1911–
    Singapore : a Virgil Tibbs mystery novel.

    I. Title.
PS3552.A455S57   1986   813'.54   85-16045
ISBN 0-396-08763-9

Author's Note

The telling of this story was only made possible by the generous cooperation and hospitality of the Singapore Police. For many weeks Deputy Commissioner Michael Chai, Deputy Assistant Commissioner Au-Yong Weng Wah, the director of the Public Relations Department, Superintendent Yeap Theam Hock, the head of the Administration and Specialist Division, Superintendent Daljit Singh Sadhu of the Traffic Division, and many other high-ranking officers were more than generous with their time, knowledge, and advice. I offer them all my most sincere and grateful thanks.

My warmest thanks are also tendered to the valued friend of both Mr. Tibbs and myself, Commander James Robenson of the Pasadena Police.

SINGAPORE

Prelude

The boy was still only seventeen when he was chosen to die. His fate was inevitable from the moment he was picked, although only a few knew of it and there was no record of any kind. In the world of terrorism the less that was written down, the better.

The Advisors were not told his name, or who he was, because it would be meaningless to them. They were only concerned with planning for the exact place and manner in which he would be used. He was a nonentity to be sacrificed with less consideration than a laboratory animal. Politics meant everything; the individual nothing.

Although very young he was already a competent driver, which was essential. He had known so little in his short life, he had no conception of what he would be forced to sacrifice. He had been judged to have been indoctrinated enough to do what would be demanded of him. That was his death warrant.

He would be made to think of himself as a volunteer destined for the highest glory. If for any reason he were to refuse, he would be swiftly eliminated; it would not do to leave anyone alive to tell of such a rebellion against authority.

At first the boy did not understand when an officer

tapped him on the shoulder and told him to board the sand-eroded vehicle that stood waiting in the dust of the unpaved street. He could only think that he had somehow done something wrong, and was about to be severely punished for it. As he rode in growing fright though the torrid, insect-infested day, his youthful mind could not even focus itself enough to let him think back and assess the events of the past few days. Although his body was developing moderately well, and he was strong for his age, he had had little to eat. Privation was the only life he knew.

He was taken into a compound and put in a mud-walled room, where he was told to wait. There for a carefully calculated time he was allowed to sit on a plain bench and imagine all sorts of possible fates that might be in store for him. When another soldier, who was older, came for him, it was a relief that his mounting uncertainty was about to be resolved.

But there were no terrors. He was received by a very important person who, despite the vast difference in their ranks, treated him as a dependable fighter for the Cause. With two others standing by as witnesses, including one of the Advisors, he was told that his commander had recommended him for a very important mission. He would have to volunteer. Overwhelmed by the authority that surrounded him, he immediately did so. He could not understand why he was being so greatly honored.

His commitment made, he was turned over to the training specialists. He was given a meal—he could not remember ever having had such a filling one—and fitted out with better clothing, as befitted a volunteer. It was far from a real uniform, but it was much better than the rags he had been wearing. To him it was something of great importance. His mind leapt ahead, and he saw himself as one of the youngest captains in the whole liberation force. From there he would rise even higher—until people who had never even seen him face to face would speak his name. To achieve that he was prepared to give all that he had, to take any risk.

For several days he was indoctrinated with fresh hatred for the enemy and trained for the task for which he had been selected.

Then he was told what he was to do. The hated enemy, the suppressors of the people, the defilers of the Prophet, were to be dealt a mortal blow. "We are at war," the Leader said, "and we are all prepared to die for victory. We are about to strike a blow that will terrify the world. The very heart of the enemy will be destroyed. You have been chosen for this great honor."

He was wildly enthusiastic until he understood that he was to die. The blow hit him harder than had been anticipated.

In the morning he was awakened and given food. In it was a drug the Advisors had supplied. It lifted his spirits, faded the reality around him, and gave him a reckless courage that seemed limitless.

The truck was relatively new, in far better condition than anything he had ever been allowed to drive. The engine started easily, the clutch did not slip, and the mufflers worked as they should. When the boy got into the driver's seat, he tried for a few stricken moments to ignore the packed load of explosives behind him. Then his mind balked, because he did not want to die.

The Advisors had foreseen that, because it had happened before. He was given a delicious drink that contained more of the drug. It took hold of him almost immediately and his fears began to vanish.

The Leader himself appeared for a final word. His encouragement and praise drove the boy to his act of self-destruction. Like a child of destiny, he drove the truck carefully through the unsuspecting city until he saw his

3

target before him. For a moment he shut his eyes, then he pointed the truck toward the entrance to the building. At the right moment he pressed down hard on the gas pedal. The truck rammed its way through the largely ornamental iron gates and careened forward.

The boy drew a great breath and yelled at the top of his voice as the wall rushed up to him faster and faster.

He lived to feel the moment of impact, then a massive explosion dissolved the truck and blasted a huge hole in the supporting wall of the building. Slowly at first, then with an increasing momentum, the structure began to collapse. The first section that fell pulled the next down with it. In less than a minute much of what had been a fine public building had been reduced almost to rubble. Some parts of it still stood, but they formed a grotesque skeleton.

So died two hundred and eighty-two people. Among those who perished was President Motamboru of Bakara, one of the most respected leaders in Africa and the true hope of his people.

Chapter One

It was almost eight o'clock in the evening when Virgil Tibbs came out of the old building that still served as the Pasadena police headquarters and turned toward the employees' parking lot to get his car. It was a cold, raw January night, with the temperature already in the low fifties and a steady drizzle of rain adding to the depressing effect of the weather.

Bone-tired from a long and exhausting day, Tibbs took refuge in his car, started the engine, and gave it a moment or two to warm up. He was in a thoroughly discouraged frame of mind. A court decision that afternoon had taken away the results of weeks of hard work on his part and set free a vicious child molester on a legal technicality. When in hell, he wondered, would they ever clean up the criminal justice system and put it in working order? He didn't know.

Trying his best to ignore the miserable weather, he turned onto the wet streets and headed for a restaurant where he could get a good hot meal. By force of habit, and regulation, he opened the glove compartment and turned on the police radio that was concealed inside. The patrol units out in the city would handle all the usual calls, but he was technically available if needed.

He had covered less than four blocks when the radio riveted his full attention. "Nine ninety-eight—Bateman Liquors. Two eleven: officer down."

Almost instantly he spun the wheel of his car, throwing it into a skid on the wet pavement. As soon as it had turned 180 degrees, he expertly recovered control and accelerated northward toward the largely black sector of the city. Nine ninety-eight—*officer needs help*—called for maximum immediate response. Only the rarely used 999—*officer in danger of his life*—carried a greater urgency.

Tibbs knew the Bateman Liquor store well; in the heart of the black area, it was a frequent crime target. The 211 code meant armed robbery. He had a Second Chance vest in the trunk of his car, but with an officer down there was no time for him to stop and put it on. He would have to take his chances as he was. During the next minute, driving as fast as he dared, he hoped to heaven that he would be recognized and that one of the new recruits wouldn't mistake him for a holdup man. He grasped his badge in his left hand as the sound of a code three siren split the wet, cold night.

When he reached the store less than two minutes later, four of the white patrol units were already on the scene. He burned rubber jerking his car to a stop on the small parking lot; then he was out and running, holding up his badge in his left hand, his gun ready in his right. Two quick, sharp shots exploded from inside the store as he reached the doorway. He caught a quick flash of an officer face up on the floor, motionless, then he darted inside and took what cover he could behind a glass showcase.

In three or four seconds he took it all in. There were two other officers inside the store; more would be forming a close perimeter just outside. The 998 call would bring every available unit; there would be plenty of manpower shortly. The immediate urgency was the officer who was down.

To his left there was a uniformed agent, who gave a quick nod to show the location of the suspect, or suspects. At his right a young officer, new to the force, was crouching in comparative safety behind a substantial wooden counter.

At that moment a face popped up at the rear of the store. It was a black man, stocking-capped, who whipped up his hands and fired a shot. The glass shattered in the case in front of Tibbs, and the thin corner post burst into fragments.

That forced the decision that Tibbs had already made. "Cover me!" he yelled, and dove forward, flat onto the floor beside the man who was already down. The palm of his hand holding his gun was sweaty, but the idea of fear was blocked out of his mind. His right arm was extended in front of his body, his gun aimed at the spot where the suspect's face had appeared. He held that position for a second or two, then he threw his left arm across the helpless man beside him and began to draw him back out of the line of fire. He knew he was being covered, but he kept his gun cocked and ready, aimed at the spot where he knew the suspect was concealed. When the man's face appeared again, he fired.

At almost the same moment from the other side of the store, another shot shook the air. Tibbs was pivoting to face his new opponent when a sudden stab of violent pain sliced his side. He felt, rather than saw, the gush of blood coming from his body. He knew that for the first time in his long service as a policeman he had been shot.

He tried to move and found that he still could. He began again to drag his fellow officer to safety when two more shots were fired, to be answered at once by the blast of a shotgun. Then acute pain took hold of him, and things began to swirl before his eyes.

He retained consciousness as he heard the noises around him. There was a rush of feet, someone screamed, "Don't shoot!" in a heavy black accent, and a scuffle erupted. Then

7

an officer he barely knew was leaning over him. "Hang tight," the man said. "Paramedics here in three or less."

Tibbs was willing to take the advice. Other, more able hands were on the job. He heard the far siren of an approaching vehicle and knew from the sound it was a paramedic ambulance. Suddenly the hard, dirty floor he was lying on became comfortable, and he had no desire at all to move. He knew that he was bleeding badly, but he almost didn't care.

A voice he knew took command in the air around him: Commander Jim Robenson, one of the top men in the department. "Give it to me, fast," he ordered.

Another voice responded: "Three of them: one dead, one down, one in custody. Two of ours down and a rent-a-cop. He's an old man, but he shot it out and hit one of them."

Tibbs felt someone bending over him, then Jim's voice came again. "Spencer Blake; he's out. And, my God, it's Virgil."

Still in the dim world of semiconsciousness, Tibbs lay still until he felt hands under him, lifting him carefully onto a litter. He was aware of the inconsequential pain when a needle was slid into his arm, then of being lifted again and moved. He was on his back now, holding his eyes shut against the bits of agony that hit him as he was carried. When the rain came down onto his face he wondered if he ought to pray. He heard Jim Robenson's voice again: "Hang on, Virg, you're in good hands now."

Then he passed out.

He awoke to find himself lying on his back on a fairly narrow, definitely hard bed. After gathering himself for the effort, he raised his head and saw that he was in a hospital room. The small amount of movement was complicated by the fact that his left side was heavily taped and his left arm liberally covered with dressings. He lay still, put his mind

8

to work, and out of the haze of sedation grasped the fact that he had been shot.

He discovered that his breathing was uncomfortable, and he had a fine assortment of various aches and pains, but as he emerged from the fog he made a self-prognosis and decided that he was going to live. Being a policeman had its risks and getting shot at was one of them. He had been lucky that this was only the first time he had been in a real shootout situation. Immediately he wanted to know more about it.

He had to content himself for almost half an hour until the door of his room was pushed in and a familiar, welcome face appeared. Bob Nakamura had been his partner for many years. As usual, he was the portrait of bucolic innocence. Slightly roundfaced and with heavy-framed glasses, he appeared to be the low man on the totem pole of a small and not too successful business. His appearance was part of his stock in trade; almost no one took him for an astute police detective until it was too late. "You should have ducked," he said.

Tibbs looked at him. "I know that now. Fill me in."

Nakamura sat beside the bed. "Three Adam Henrys from south central L.A. hit Bateman's. All male, Negro, twenty to twenty-five, on parole. They charged in with guns out and went for the clerk who just had time to hit the silent alarm. When the first unit responded, shots were fired. Spence Blake took a slug in the chest, but he had his Second Chance on and he's okay. His partner put out the nine ninety-eight."

"Did we get them?"

Nakamura adjusted his glasses. "One in the jail ward at U.C.M.C., one in custody, one dead. On our side there's you and a rent-a-cop who's going to make it. An old World War Two vet who hadn't forgotten how to shoot. Incidentally, you're now a mongrel. There's been a run on blood lately, after the latest AIDS scare, so you've got some of my good Japanese blood inside that black hide of yours."

"Thanks," Tibbs said. "Maybe now I can eat with chopsticks."

Nakamura stood up. "I'm glad it wasn't worse, Virg," he said. "When I first heard . . . " He took Tibbs's right hand and held it a moment before he left.

After he had gone, the pain in Tibbs's side began a steady pounding. He stared at the ceiling, pressed his lips together, and thought his thanks that it hadn't been worse. He could have been in I.C.U., or the morgue. But he was still glad he had answered the *officer needs help* call; he couldn't have lived with himself if he hadn't.

Chapter Two

Three days later they let him go home. By hospital regulations he was taken outside in a wheelchair although he could walk without too much pain. The dressings on his side and arm had been reduced; his worst discomfort was a persistent itching that he could do nothing to relieve. His car had been brought around, and he was able to drive as long as he took it carefully.

When he put a key into the lock of his apartment door and opened it, he took a quick look around to verify that everything was just as he had left it. Once he was inside, he took off his short-barreled Smith and Wesson in its holster and put it in its usual place, out of sight. He hung his jacket in the closet that held most of his wardrobe and then turned to the slender pile of his mail. For the hundredth time he allowed himself a tiny flame of hope, but it flickered out as soon as he had checked the few envelopes. Miriam had not written. He did not really expect that she ever would, but the thin possibility gave him something to hope for each time he came home from work.

He went into his compact kitchenette and fixed himself a drink. The sun was not long over the yardarm, but he knew he deserved it. He had survived, and self-congratulation was in order. He turned to his record library, looking for something that would suit the mood he was in: something peaceful and yet with substance; something that would ease the persistent pain in his side. He chose Debussy's *La Mer* and put it on his stereo. As the soothing sounds of a great orchestra began to fill the small apartment, he sat down with his drink and reminded himself that he was free of all duties until he had a complete medical discharge. It was a welcome respite, especially after the outcome of his most recent major case.

As it always did, William Holt-Rymers's radiant painting of Tibbs's nudist friend Linda lifted his spirits. It had been their gift to him, and he treasured it. She was a lovely blue-eyed blonde, whose perfectly formed breasts seemed to epitomize everything that was ideal about young womanhood. His memories of Sun Valley Lodge, where she lived, were interrupted when the telephone rang.

He turned down the music and reached for the phone. Very few people had his private number; most of them were his police colleagues.

"Tibbs," he said.

A voice he did not recognize came over the line. "Mr. Tibbs, my name is Jim Reynolds. I'd like to see you for a few minutes if you don't mind."

"What about?"

"I'd rather tell you when I see you."

"I'm sorry, but I'm just out of the hospital."

"I know, but this is a matter of considerable urgency."

"You'd better give me a clue," Tibbs said.

"I'm with the government."

The silence across the phone line was heavy. Tibbs had heard that innocent-sounding statement too often before not to know what it probably meant.

"You have I.D.?" he asked.

"Yes."

Reluctantly, Tibbs gave up the privacy he so urgently wanted. "All right, then."

12

"Thank you. In about twenty minutes. I have the address." Reynolds hung up.

As Tibbs sipped his drink and waited, he was almost grateful he had been shot: no one now could force any work on him he didn't want. He had a deeply ingrained resentment of being forced into anything. It had been born in his early childhood when his father had had to explain to him the difference in his heritage.

For the first time he had understood why his mother had not been allowed to get on a bus when there had been empty seats and why they never went to the regular theaters and restaurants. That night he had wanted to die, until he had heard his father crying because of what he had had to tell his boy. Father and son, they had curled up together and shared their love.

He threw off those bitter memories and remembered how things had changed for the better. When his parents had come to see him graduate from the University of California, out of his small savings he had sent them first-class tickets. On that supporting thought he kept a better frame of mind until the doorbell rang.

When he looked through the fisheye viewer, he saw an I.D. card being held up for his inspection. He opened the door.

To his surprise he had two visitors instead of one. The man who had displayed his I.D. was slightly over six feet; his body obviously was that of a person who kept himself in shape. His custom-tailored suit was expensive, but subdued. His mid-blond hair was carefully cut and still full. The man with him was an inch or two shorter, but equally well dressed in a conservative sports jacket and slacks. Together they were an impressive pair.

"Mr. Tibbs," the taller man said, "I'm Jim Reynolds. This is Bill Conners. Thank you for seeing us."

"Please come in," Tibbs said.

As soon as the door was closed, both men held out I.D.s

for his inspection. Tibbs examined each of them carefully before handing them back.

"Sit down," he said. "I don't have very much to offer you—"

Conners politely cut him off. "It isn't necessary, thank you."

That told Tibbs he was the senior man of the two, but Reynolds began the conversation. "I'm sorry to disturb you," he began, "but we needed to see you right away. I hope you're feeling much better."

"Some," Virgil answered.

Reynolds came to the point. "Mr. Tibbs, some months ago we had a luncheon meeting with your chief. Were you aware of that?"

"No."

"It concerned Mrs. Miriam Motamboru."

That name sent a sudden shock the length of Tibbs's spine, but he carefully concealed it.

Conners took up the conversation. "I believe you know that President Motamboru of Bakara was one of the most capable heads of state in Africa. He was also fearlessly honest."

"I know his reputation," Tibbs said, his voice a little tight. "I admired him very much."

"He managed to establish a successful democracy in a very difficult area," Conners continued. "That automatically made him some powerful enemies. You know about the Russian efforts to penetrate into Africa, and the Cuban troops that Castro sent there."

Tibbs nodded.

Reynolds took over. "Motamboru was a realist; he knew the risks he had to take. They didn't deter him, but he was very concerned about his family, particularly when a lot of hate propaganda began to be aimed at his wife. I haven't personally met her, but I understand she's quite remarkable."

"That's true," Tibbs agreed. "She holds a doctorate from the Sorbonne and speaks several languages. Also, she's exceptionally attractive."

Reynolds indicated he already knew that. "When Bakara began to come under increasing attack, Motamboru asked us to grant temporary asylum to his wife and children. The President personally agreed."

Conners picked it up. "You know what happened, but you may not know how you were selected. We got your name from a computer that can locate police officers and other law enforcement personnel who have unusual capabilities. If we need a man able to speak both Turkish and Russian, we can find him if he exists. This time we needed a very special peace officer to pose as Mrs. Motamboru's husband. He had to be well educated, resourceful, and, most of all, totally trustworthy."

"And," Reynolds added, "he had to be black. You were checked out down to the ground before we decided that you were our man. We set up a safe house in Pasadena and moved Mrs. Motamboru here with her children." Reynolds loosened up a little. "I understand you learned about all this rather dramatically." He smiled as he spoke.

"I did," Tibbs said. "I came home after a short vacation and found this place completely empty; stripped to the walls. I called the watch commander, who sent me to an elegant home in the high-rent district. A very stunning woman answered the door. She told me that she was Mrs. Tibbs. She said her husband was not at home, but I was welcome to leave a message. That's how I met my supposed wife."

"I would have liked to have seen that," Conners said, "but now let's get down to business. Mrs. Motamboru spoke highly of you. She said you were a complete gentleman and a fine temporary father to her two children. I hope you enjoyed the assignment."

"I did," Tibbs admitted. "Particularly since she's both a

15

delightful lady and a remarkable cook. I never had such meals in my life."*

There was a pause before Conners asked, "Do you know how her husband was killed?"

Tibbs nodded. "A suicide truck bomb smashed into the capitol building."

"That's right. The suicide driver was a young Arab, but the operation was Soviet directed, and two-pronged. The first objective was to kill Motamboru. The second was to destroy his wife. She was much too popular for them in her own country."

Conners saw Tibbs's face and added quickly to that, "They didn't want to kill her and make her a martyr. They preferred to fix it so that she could never carry on in her husband's place."

By careful effort Tibbs kept his voice calm. "What did they do?" he asked.

Reynolds answered him. "When she fled her country, as she eventually had to, they enticed her to Singapore. Never mind how, we'll give you that later. She's there now, being held in the women's prison on a murder charge."

"*Murder,*" Tibbs said. "I can't believe it!"

"She was framed, we know that, but it was expertly done. There's very strong evidence against her. Strong enough that she could be found guilty and hanged. Singapore is very strict about such things."

Despite his complexion, Tibbs's face almost turned ashen. "Do you mean hanged, literally?" he asked.

"Yes," Conners answered. "On the gallows, tied hand and foot, the noose around her neck, then the drop."

It was deliberately brutal, and Tibbs knew it. "What do you want me to do?" he asked.

"A senior representative of the State Department saw her a few days ago," Conners said. "She's convinced that

---

* For further details, see *Then Came Violence.*

16

if anyone alive can get her out of her present jam, you're the one."

The silence was palpable. Tibbs folded his hands and pressed his fingers together so tightly the circulation was cut off.

Reynolds laid it out. "As soon as you can travel, we want you to go there, to see what you can do for her. We'll arrange a leave for you."

Virgil's dark eyes were deep with thought. "If I go barging into the Singapore Police's territory, interfering with their work, they're going to hate my guts before I get off the plane."

"You'll be in the middle, we know that," Conners said. "However, we've already talked with the Singapore Police. They're willing to extend you every courtesy."

"We can't interfere publicly with the internal affairs of another country," Reynolds added, "and Singapore is a country. But they've agreed to let you conduct your own investigation, under their supervision."

Tibbs forced thoughts of Miriam Motamboru out of his mind. "I can't," he said. "There's no way I can go to Singapore, where I don't know the language or the laws, and do an investigation with no police authority. My position would be impossible."

"That's all true," Reynolds agreed. "You'll be in a difficult situation. Politically it's a very hot potato. But you have an excuse; you're Mrs. Motamboru's personal friend, come to help her if you can."

"We believe you think enough of the lady to be willing to do this," Conners added. "Also you'll be doing something for your country. Some of us still consider that important."

"When?" Tibbs asked.

"We talked with Dr. Steinglas at the hospital. He feels you'll be okay to travel by the weekend."

Tibbs's mind was churning with images of Miriam Motamboru. During the weeks they had lived in the same house, he had inevitably been greatly attracted to her. He had kept hands off, physically and mentally, while he had been her guardian. After the death of her husband, he had hoped that someday he might see her again. Now the electrifying possibility was before him, but with almost impossible strings attached.

Reynolds produced a large envelope and handed it over. "That will give you most of the background you'll need," he said. "Come to the Federal Building on Wilshire Thursday at three. You'll be briefed at that time."

Tibbs looked squarely at Conners. "Give it to me in the clear," he said. "How bad is it for her, and what possible chance do I have?"

"You'll be up against a powerful hostile organization," Conners answered. "The people who killed her husband. As to what you may be able to do, that's up to you. Just remember that a helluva lot more than Mrs. Motamboru's future will be in your hands on this one."

Chapter Three

By Wednesday morning Virgil Tibbs felt well enough to stop in at his office. He was officially on sick leave, in line of duty, but he had certain matters to clear up.

When Bob Nakamura, his partner, came in, Tibbs looked up. "Shut the door, will you," he asked.

Nakamura gave him a sharp look. As far as he could remember, it was the first time in their long association that Tibbs had ever greeted him like that. He complied and then sat down. "Let's have it, Virg," he said.

"I've had a couple of official visitors," Tibbs began.

"Local?" Nakamura asked.

"No. Feds."

"In our line of work?"

"Not exactly."

"If they were from the Head Shed, I can make a guess."

"Go ahead."

"Something to do with Miriam."

"You've got it," Tibbs acknowledged. "Since you were in on it from the beginning, I don't have to clam up. Also I'm going to need some help."

"Ask and ye shall receive."

"Not for publication, they want to spring me to go to Singapore. Miriam's in a jam there."

Nakamura was quick. "It sounds as if they might need a fall guy."

"That thought crossed my mind," Tibbs agreed, "but I've got damn little choice in the matter."

"How about your job?"

"I'll know more in a few minutes; I'm going up to see Jim Robenson. I may have to leave here this week. If so, I won't be able to attend to a lot of things. My apartment . . ."

"I'll look after it for you. No problem." Nakamura pulled a piece of paper in front of him and began to make notes. "Utility bills?"

"I'll leave you some cash and a power of attorney. I also owe a little on my car. Otherwise I'm clear."

"What about your car?"

"You might start it up once in a while. I don't know how long I'll be gone."

Nakamura wrote. "What else?"

"Just use your own judgment. I'll keep in touch."

Nakamura shook his head. "Virg, this sounds pretty damn serious. Keep your head down this time."

Tibbs looked at his partner. "Thanks, Bob." Then he picked up his desk phone and called the fourth floor.

Commander James Robenson, one of the four top brass of the department, had come up through the ranks by means of a near legendary career. As a sergeant he had once ordered a top mobster and his entourage to get out of his city, and had made it stick. There was a plentiful supply of stories about Robenson in all of the various divisions; most of them true.

When Virgil Tibbs arrived at his office, Robenson got up himself to shut the door. "No calls," he said to his secretary. Then he settled behind his desk.

Tibbs came directly to the point. "Jim, a few months ago I was involved in a special assignment."

"I know all about it," Robenson said. "It involved an important foreign lady."

"Yes. Have you had any callers from Washington lately?"

The commander nodded. "The chief's away and they came to see me. I've got the picture, but I don't altogether like it. First, because we need you here. Secondly, I think you're being set up in a no-win situation."

"I agree with that." Tibbs showed a rare flash of displeasure. "But what choice do I have? I like the lady very much, I don't deny that, but they put it to me that it's for the benefit of the country. I'm a cop, not a diplomat."

"Don't forget, Virgil, how many times you have to be both. I've had visitors, as you said, also a high-powered call from their Head Shed in Washington. Do you want my guess?"

"Yes."

"Having Mrs. Motamboru in custody on a one-eighty-seven rap has to be a major embarrassment to our colleagues in Singapore. But they can't just let her go; you can see why. You might be their way out."

Robenson had the ability to make good decisions quickly when they were needed. "Since you're already on sick leave, as of now you're excused for an indefinite period. Come back when you can. Is there anything else I can do for you?"

"No, Jim, and thanks a lot."

Virgil drove back to his apartment wondering when he would be back once more in the accustomed pattern of his life. He liked his work, but nothing, he knew, stood still indefinitely.

Five minutes before three on Thursday, Tibbs finally found a parking spot at the Federal Building and went inside. He was wearing a charcoal-gray suit that would have fit better without the dressings that had been changed that morning. He carried a thin, flexible briefcase in which he had a long legal pad and several pens; otherwise he was unencumbered.

He consulted the directory, took an express elevator up, and presented himself at a reception desk. There he went through a security check. As soon as it was over, Jim Reynolds came out and took him inside.

The room into which he was shown had been designed for briefing purposes. It was not large, but there were several chairs with widened right-hand armrests for taking notes. Instead of being lined up in rows, they were grouped in a rough circle. There was also a blackboard and a projection screen rolled up against the ceiling.

Reynolds introduced him to a fairly short, stocky man somewhere in his mid-forties. "I'd like you to meet Glenn Hopjoy," he said. "Glenn is with the State Department. This is Virgil Tibbs."

Hopjoy shook hands calmly and then motioned toward the chairs. "Let's sit down," he suggested. "How are you feeling?"

"Reasonably well, considering."

"Can you get around all right?"

"As long as I take it easy."

There were two other men present who were not introduced and who remained in the background. When the small party had settled down, Hopjoy asked, "How do you stand right now?"

"I'm on leave from my job," Tibbs answered, "for an indefinite period. My partner will look after my personal affairs while I'm gone."

"On the basis of what Jim Reynolds told you."

Tibbs shifted his position a little. "No, of course not," he replied. "As soon as Reynolds left, I called a close friend I have in the FBI. I asked for some background information on him and a confirmation of his status."

Hopjoy's eyebrows lifted, but his voice was easy as he asked, "Where is this man based?"

"Washington. I also asked for any further unclassified information he could give me. I wasn't about to ship out to Singapore on the unsupported word of two men I didn't know."

Hopjoy was satisfied. "Okay, Mr. Tibbs; I would have done the same thing."

There was a brief lull. While Hopjoy took his time, the others remained silent. Finally he spoke again. "Mr. Tibbs, you're qualified for a secret clearance; it's already being processed. I may step it up a grade if it seems desirable."

Bending down, he extracted a large manila envelope from his briefcase. "For the time being you'll be a temporary employee of the government, at the GS fourteen level," he continued. "That should meet your financial needs. I've had some I.D.s made up for you. One is for normal use, which means that you use it when you think it desirable."

"I dislike people who flash the badge," Tibbs said.

Hopjoy ignored that. "I'm also providing you with another I.D. If you use it, it will get a lot of attention *very* quickly, so don't produce it unless you mean business." Hopjoy looked up. "Ray, see if you can scare us up some coffee."

One of the two silent men who sat in the back got up and left the room.

"A couple of more things," Hopjoy continued. "Don't advertise this, but we'll meet all of your reasonable expenses for as long as necessary, that's win or lose. In that envelope you'll find some documents that may help you. There's a copy of a letter to Mr. Arthur Sim, the deputy commissioner of the Singapore Police. You'll also find a round-trip ticket to Singapore on Japan Air Lines. Since you're recuperating from work-related injuries, I put you in first class."

Tibbs was listening carefully, but he said nothing.

"Now on a different topic," Hopjoy went on. "As of this moment, Motamboru's whole regime in Bakara is under heavy fire. He made it a point to develop younger people to follow after him. Many of them are outstanding, but they don't yet have his experience, or his charisma."

Tibbs remained quiet.

"That whole region of Africa is loaded with Marxists, Russian 'advisors,' and trained terrorists: some from Cuba, some from Libya, and quite a few from Iran. They set out to eliminate Motamboru and succeeded. They're now making a concerted attack on Bakara, for several reasons. First, it's a democracy with better food, better housing, and better living conditions than they have in surrounding nations. Naturally they don't like that."

He paused for a moment. "Secondly, there are certain mineral assets being developed by us in cooperation with the Bakara government that we rather urgently need. Their loss would be a serious setback to our defense posture.

"As you know, Mrs. Motamboru is a remarkable person. She is quite capable of carrying on for her late husband, and she is a very popular figure. The opposition is determined not to allow her to take his place."

The man who had left the room returned with five cups of coffee on an impromptu tray. He also had some powdered creamer, a box half full of sugar cubes, and some plastic spoons. For a minute or two everyone helped himself, then Hopjoy continued.

"Jim told you that Mrs. Motamboru is in jail in Singapore, awaiting trial on a murder charge. It's a very serious situation. There's no endless appeal process in Singapore the way we have here. If a person is convicted of a capital offense, there's an automatic appeal to the high court with three judges sitting. If that fails, the accused can appeal to the Privy Council in England. Singapore is an independent nation, but it follows the British legal system. The Privy Council is unlikely to interfere. After that there's a final appeal for clemency to the President of the Republic. He can commute the sentence, but usually doesn't. That's the end of the legal road. As of now, there's no denying that the lady's in a very tough spot."

"How did it happen?" Tibbs asked.

Hopjoy hesitated for a moment or two. "It's all in the envelope," he said. Then he added, "I expected you to tell me you were sure she was innocent. I hope to God she is, because if she hangs, it'll be a major victory for the communists in her part of the world. She's a symbol, you see. If she goes, then the whole image of democracy in that part of Africa goes with her."

Tibbs tried to drink some of his coffee, but his hand shook.

Hopjoy noted it and softened up a little. "May I call you Virgil?" he asked.

"Please."

"I don't want you to think, Virgil, that we're just letting the lady dangle. I'm sorry—that's a bad metaphor. We've been in diplomatic contact with the Singapore government. They understand our concern, but they can't just let her go: if they did, the propaganda uproar would be disastrous. This is where you come in. Do you know anything about Singapore?"

"Very little."

"It's a very small nation in a highly strategic location. Seventy-five percent of her population is Chinese, and no informed person in his right mind has ever accused those people of being dumb. It's possibly the cleanest city in the world, and one of the most modern. If you've been thinking about bamboo shacks, forget it; that's like trying to find Indians on Manhattan Island."

"I can't speak Chinese," Tibbs said.

25

"You don't need to. The Singapore Police is made up of Chinese, Malays, Indonesians, Muslims, Sikhs, Hindus—you name it—but they're a thoroughly professional organization, and every sworn member speaks English."

"I have a friend there," Tibbs volunteered. "Inspector Lee. We met through the International Police Association."

"That could be an important plus. You can expect that they'll treat you with great courtesy, that's their way. But it doesn't mean that they accept you as a blood brother. If you want their real respect, you'll have to earn it."

"Can you tell me," Tibbs asked with forced calm, "the circumstances of Mrs. Motamboru's arrest?"

Hopjoy took his time before he answered. "It's all in the packet, as I said. Briefly, Mrs. Motamboru was staying on the twenty-second floor of the Crossroads Hotel, one of the newest in Singapore. Because of her position, she was permitted to carry a small weapon. A man was admitted to her suite. A few minutes later an important call from the embassy was put through. When there was no answer, the hotel security people went up and knocked two or three times. Then they opened the door with a passkey.

"They found the male visitor lying dead on the floor. He'd been shot once through the center of the forehead. Mrs. Motamboru's gun was lying near him. She's an expert shot; her husband insisted that she learn. Two maids were working close by; one of them was vacuuming the corridor carpeting just outside. Both of them swear that no one else either went in or out of the suite, and there's only one door.

"When the rooms were searched by the security people, no one else was there. The Crossroads Hotel is a smooth-sided building with no possible way to climb up or down without elaborate gear. The suite faces Orchard Road, a main thoroughfare, so anyone trying to go in or out of a window would have been seen."

"Time of day?" Tibbs asked.

"Three-thirty P.M. Weather bright and clear."

"The door was locked?"

"Yes. The guest-room doors all lock automatically. Nothing was blocking the sill."

"Mrs. Motamboru's statement?"

"She claims to have been rendered unconscious in some way. When she came to, the security people were just coming in."

Hopjoy got up. "That's it. Unravel this one for us, Virgil, if you can, and the President will thank you personally."

Tibbs stood up and picked up his briefcase. "I'll do my best," he promised.

Chapter Four

In the very early hours of the morning, well before the first streaks of dawn were due to show in the sky, most of the more than two million inhabitants of Singapore lay asleep. A warm, gentle trade wind was blowing off the Indian Ocean, across the Straits of Malacca and Singapore Island, toward a timeless destination somewhere over the vastness of the South China Sea.

In one of the high-rise towers of the Toa Payoh Housing Estate, Madam Wee Lai Chan was lying in bed beside her husband. For some reason sleep was eluding her; she was drifting from partial slumber to semiconsciousness and back again like the very gentle swell of a placid ocean. In her mind she was retracing for the thousandth time their good fortune in securing the tiny apartment in which they lived with the four children she had borne and who would care and provide for her and her husband in their old age. Two sons and two daughters were not as gratifying as four sons would have been, but someone had to have daughters if there were to be brides for all the fine sons. Someone would have to bear their children. Fortune had been very good to her, especially since she had known severe privation in her early life and the bitter cold that so often racked the northwestern part of the Chinese mainland. Now she lived less than a hundred miles from the equator and would never be cold again.

When she became even more awake, she got up as quietly as she could to visit the toilet. Then she walked softly in her bare feet to look in the small room where her children, the oldest only eight, were wrapped in their innocent dreams. In the darkness very little was visible, but something impelled her to look more closely. As silently as she could, she entered the room. A few seconds later her frantic screams rang throughout the building.

As they continued with no letup, people awoke, babies began to cry, and lights appeared on four different floors. Someone picked up a telephone and dialed 999.

In the Khe Bong Neighborhood Police Post, Block 89, Lorong 2, Inspector Cheng Boon Lai answered the call. At that hour of the morning he expected it would be about a pregnant woman whose time had come sooner than expected and who needed immediate help. "Police. Inspector Cheng," he said in Mandarin, the most common language of the area.

"There's a woman screaming on our floor," a man's voice told him.

The inspector's expectation seemed confirmed. "Location?" he asked.

Fortunately the police post was in the same building. Cheng sent Constables Sung and Hassan to investigate. He realized that he might save a little time by calling an ambulance at once, but his constables would let him know very quickly if one was needed.

Within minutes Constable Hassan reported by radio in English, the only language common to all members of the department. "A child has been murdered," he said without preamble. "Full assistance is needed."

Inspector Cheng notified headquarters at once, where the word was almost immediately passed to the Scene of

29

the Crime Unit, which always responded in such situations. Medical help was also quickly dispatched. Then Cheng turned over his command to his duty sergeant in order to take personal control until the reinforcements arrived.

In the building, Cheng found a scene of near chaos. The hall outside the apartment was jammed with people determined to miss nothing, but the power of his position enabled him to worm his way in. Constable Hassan was controlling the front door with considerable difficulty; his partner was doing his best to calm and quiet Madam Wee. She was close to hysterics; her husband stood by her in a state of shock. Sung nodded his head toward the small room where the children slept. Three of them, silent and stunned, stood together in the little family room in their night clothes, waiting to be told what to do.

The inspector entered the children's bedroom, being very careful not to destroy any evidence as he did so. He wanted first to verify what Hassan had told him. He did not doubt his man, but he well knew that a sudden first impression could easily be wrong. Perhaps the child was only badly hurt.

He did not need to look for long. The little girl was dead, her throat gashed wide open. A hot red mist boiled up before Cheng's eyes. He had children of his own, including a daughter of the same age. His experience told him that the father was probably responsible, but someone was going to pay with his life for the terrible thing he had done to that innocent child.

By the time Cheng came back into the family room, white police cars with flashing lights had begun to fill the available spaces before the high-rise structure. The officer in charge was Deputy Superintendent Dalip Singh, tall and impressive in his immaculate turban. At the crime scene he was met by Cheng, who very swiftly outlined the few available facts. Singh had seen many cases of violent death; quite frequently the victim was someone who would not be sorely missed, but a child was different. When he reached the death scene and stooped for a closer look at the innocent little victim, a tear rolled down each of his cheeks.

There was a fresh stir in the hallway as the medical people came hurrying in, their trip clearly of no use to the small victim. The nurse did her job, then rose to her feet and pronounced the little girl dead.

That was the signal for Singh to bring his own people in. They quickly blocked off the crime scene and the nearby area with tapes. Then they set to work as a smoothly functioning unit to make an intensive examination of the apartment. Singh and his team had an excellent record. Only the week before, a murderer had gone to the gallows because Singh had noticed two very tiny parallel tears in a piece of discarded canvas and had correctly read their meaning.

More police support arrived. A full homicide team headed by recently promoted Assistant Superintendent Lee Kong Ho began a systematic examination of all possible witnesses. Lee, fast and efficient in deploying his forces, assigned four men to interview the occupants of every unit in the same wing. Four more officers were to take the names and unit numbers of all persons who wished to leave the building; no one was allowed to go until he had been interviewed.

Next Lee turned to a woman police officer he had brought with him. "Take those three children aside," he directed. "Be very gentle with them, but keep them away from their parents and don't allow anyone to talk to them unless I authorize it."

Finally Lee turned to Inspector Cheng, who was standing by. "Do you know this family?" he asked.

"Yes," Cheng answered. "The husband, Tan Khin Peow, is a member of the Block Committee. I've spoken with him on many occasions."

"What's his job?"

"He's an engineer with the Leong Shipyards."

"What's he like?"

"He's a good family man and a respected block leader." Because they knew each other well, he did not hesitate to add to that. "Obviously he's the prime suspect, but he's always shown great pride in his children. He's even-tempered and sober. I just can't see him killing a completely innocent child, especially *his* child."

"What's your theory?"

"My best guess at the moment would be an intruder, although the door was locked."

"Are you sure?"

"Yes. When my men responded to the call, they heard screaming inside. They tried the door and it was locked. Before they could use their master key, the husband let them in."

"What was his condition?"

"He could hardly speak and moved like a man in a trance."

"Where his hands wet or damp?"

"Sir?"

"Did you men notice if he had recently washed his hands?"

"I don't know; I'll check that with Hassan immediately."

Instead of waiting for the answer, Lee turned to Madam Wee, the mother of the murdered child. He was careful to bow his respects before he spoke. "In the depths of my heart I feel acutely your deep distress," he said in formal Mandarin.

The bereaved woman lowered her head. "You do us undeserved honor," she answered. Her speech told Lee that she was an educated woman; she might even have been to the university. Under the circumstances she was managing to control herself well.

"Fix your mind upon the Compassionate One," Lee said. "Let the vast goodness that radiates from Him comfort you in your grief."

Tears she could no longer control rolled down Madam Wee's smooth cheeks. It was very hard for her to speak, but she managed a few words. "Sir, we are Christians, not Buddhists."

Lee took his time; his genuine empathy with the suffering woman made his job much harder. He reshaped his words to try to give her some modicum of comfort. "Then you know that at this moment your child is in the loving arms of her Savior, the One who welcomed the little children to come to Him."

Madam Wee lowered her head. "You are a man of great compassion," she said. In the circular way of Chinese speech, that told Lee that his subject was ready to allow him to ask what he must.

In his most careful manner he began a brief interrogation. "When you closed the door for the night, who else was here in your apartment?"

"My husband and our four children." She could not hold back a heartbreaking sob.

"Could anyone else have been here?"

Madam Wee shook her head. "We had no guests, and there is no place for anyone to hide."

That was probably true, but Lee made a mental note to check. Sometimes there were hiding places people never suspected.

"I don't want to distress you more than necessary, but I must ask: Does your husband have any enemies, anyone who might attack his family?"

Madam Wee shook her head.

"Does he belong to a secret society?"

"No." It was so soft Lee could hardly hear her.

"Is there anyone who might wish you . . . to be very unhappy?"

This time the bereaved woman shook her head, both to answer the question and to try and free herself from the ordeal of the interview.

It was clear that she was in no condition to answer any more questions, so Lee thanked her and then turned toward Constable Hassan, who was waiting.

"We have a place for the mother and children to stay," Hassan said.

"Then take them there immediately."

"Yes, sir."

Lee watched while the children and their mother were escorted out. Silently the watchers in the corridor opened up a place for them; a few of the older people bowed to them as much as the crowded space permitted.

Increasingly he was sure that Cheng had been right. There had been no guests in the little apartment; there were few if any places for a possible intruder to hide, and the door had been locked. Tan almost had to have been responsible for the death of his own child. On the surface, it was the only explanation that fit the known facts.

Lee was an expert in detecting lies and incomplete testimony. As he seated Tan in front of him and began his routine questioning, he was confident he would get the truth from the man. He began with every outward show of sympathy and compassion. Fifteen minutes later Lee ceased his interrogation. If he had learned anything at all it was that Tan had no apparent motive whatever for the killing of his daughter. He was successfully employed. He seemed to have no gambling or other pressing debts. Although his marriage had been arranged, he was deeply in love with his wife and family. His grief appeared in every way to be genuine.

Lee retreated to the neighborhood police post to confer with Singh and Inspector Cheng. After the three policemen went into an inner room and closed the door, Superintendent Singh was the first to speak. "We'll have to wait for the lab reports on the evidence we've gathered—perhaps the vacuuming will turn up something. Otherwise we have nothing at all."

"The murder weapon?" Cheng made it a question.

"A knife was used, but we have not recovered it. Nothing appears to be missing from the kitchen. I will ask Madam Wee to confirm that as soon as I decently can, but one thing is sure: the weapon isn't in the apartment. The widest range over which it could have been dropped or thrown from a window has also been thoroughly searched."

"Could anyone have picked it up and taken it away?" Lee asked, more for the sake of thoroughness than because he thought it likely.

"Close to impossible," Singh answered. "A passerby would have had to pick up a knife that was certainly bloody, conceal it somehow on his person, and then leave the area totally unseen—all within a few yards of a police post. An honest citizen would report it at once; a thief would know the desperate risk he would be taking for an object of little value."

"So," Cheng said, "the father can hardly be a suspect."

Singh turned to Lee. "You've had wide experience in family disputes and violence," he said. "What's your opinion?"

"I interviewed the father very carefully. I was aware of his good reputation, but that means little under the circumstances. Still, I detected no indications of guilt."

"Look," Cheng said. "I can't understand several things. First, where is the motive? We have a happy family facing no problems. There are no known enemies. Second, assuming it was someone from the outside, how did he gain access to the building, reach the seventh floor, go down the hall, open the door, commit the crime, and then make his escape without being seen?"

"It could have been someone who already lives in the building," Singh said. "Someone who has a known right to be there."

"Our canvass may turn up something," Lee said. "I have ten men on the job and have sent for more. With luck something will be discovered. But if nothing at all is found within the next few hours, then we are going to be in trouble."

Deputy Commissioner Arthur Sim of the Singapore Police sat behind his well-organized desk in a deeply clouded mood. True to the traditions of his upbringing he did not let it show, but to the other men in the room it was as clear as if the moving finger had written it on the wall.

Four of his top division heads were present at his request. Also there, despite an enervating lack of sleep, was Lee Kong Ho, better known to his Western friends as Roger. As a newly promoted assistant superintendent, he was very much the junior member of the party. Because of that he was making a careful effort to be as inconspicuous as possible in the presence of so many of the high and the mighty.

"Gentlemen," the deputy commissioner began, "a fresh complication has been added to our lives, one which, unfortunately, we cannot avoid." At such times he tended to be a bit formal. His rank entitled him to the privilege.

"I don't need to remind you that having Madam Motamboru here under the existing circumstances is a major embarrassment for us. If she would only have sense enough to plead self defense, the matter could be handled. However, so far she has refused."

Superintendent Pandian Subramaniam, who commanded the Homicide Division, felt strongly on that matter. As he spoke, his black eyes were remarkably alive in his dark-skinned face. "The story she insists on telling is insulting," he declared. "How she could possibly expect us to believe it is beyond my understanding."

"Let us say that Madam is confused," Sim suggested. At that a very senior chief superintendent nodded his agreement. The implication was clear that an improvement could be expected.

Sim looked at Lee, who very much wished that he hadn't. "I know that you've been up most of the night," the deputy commissioner said, "but I would like to know first-hand about the child homicide at the Toa Payoh Housing Estate. I'm sure we're all concerned."

Organizing himself quickly, Lee gave a careful, precise account of the Tan child's murder, how it had been discovered, and the actions that had been taken up to that time. When he finished, he was rewarded with an approving nod from the deputy commissioner himself.

"I'm sure the investigation will continue with full efficiency," Sim said. "Despite the fact that it may not be an easy one."

Subramaniam spoke again. "I trust we'll be allowed to get on with it, free of outside interference."

"That, of course, is why I've called us together," the deputy commissioner declared. "I'm sure that we're all aware that a visitor is on his way, one with whom we will have to contend."

"I wish that immigration could find some convenient way to keep him out of the country," Subramaniam said.

"Let's not waste time on vain hopes," Sim replied. "His name is Virgil Tibbs. He is an American homicide expert from a small but well-regarded department in California. I understand that he is a close friend of Madam's, under proper circumstances of course. The American government has seen fit to second him to us and has requested our cooperation."

He looked once more at Lee. "Since you know him, perhaps you will tell us a little about this Mr. Tibbs."

"I spent several days with him in Pasadena," Lee said. "I now regard him as my friend."

That was a strong statement and was accepted as such.

"He is a very good policeman, there is no doubt of that," Lee continued. "His track record, as the Americans say, is exceptional and I could see why." He looked directly at the deputy commissioner. "Also, sir, I'm pleased to add that he is a gentleman."

In that company it was an ultimate endorsement. In making it Lee was automatically accepting responsibility for whatever Tibbs might do in Singapore. He knew it, but he did not flinch from his duty as he saw it.

"That is very welcome information," Sim said. "Obviously Mr. Tibbs is a complication I wish we could have avoided. I have the fullest confidence in our own people, and the intrusion of someone from an outside jurisdiction is likely to upset a good many of them. But it cannot be helped, so it must be endured. He is to receive every courtesy and as much cooperation as circumstances may require."

"It occurs to me," Pandian Subramaniam, the chief superintendent, said, "that Mr. Tibbs's visit could serve a useful purpose. Since he is a close friend of Madam, perhaps he will be able to persuade her to be sensible and plead self defense. If he succeeds, we will be relieved of a very sticky problem. On the other hand, if he fails, he will become what the Americans call the fall guy. The blame will rest solidly on him and not on us."

No one chose to comment on that.

"How long is he going to stay?" someone asked.

"I have no idea," Sim answered. "Since he is a gentle-man, I'm sure he will not overstay his welcome."

"In that case," Subramaniam said a little bitterly, "he should have had sense enough not to come at all."

Chapter Five

As the huge Japan Air Lines 747 winged its way steadily over the South China Sea, Virgil Tibbs did his best to sit quietly and relax, but too many disturbing thoughts churning in his mind kept him from enjoying the rich amenities of the first-class section. He'd spent the night in Japan in a very comfortable hotel, but sleep had eluded him. The pains in his side where he had been shot were having another go at him and kept him from any real rest. Once when he had dozed off, he'd popped wide awake again, suddenly fearful that he would be late in getting to his office, his ingrained habits upset by the jet lag.

A stewardess came to his seat, gave him a warm smile, and set up his tray table for still another meal. She was an attractive Japanese who had the traditional grace of the Orient about her. He assumed she could speak two or three languages; it would be part of her job on long international flights.

He was not in the mood for a lavish lunch, but the carts that were being wheeled up the aisle left no doubt that one was forthcoming. Very shortly a bowl of soup was set on the service plate before him while another stewardess poured him a glass of wine. Almost seven miles below, the clear and brilliant sun glinted off a seemingly endless spread of water.

Taking himself in hand, Tibbs tried to push the worries of his assignment out of his mind. They would only interfere with his efficiency, and if ever in his life he had to be at his best, this would be the time. He tried the soup and found it delicious.

Two hours later, when the giant aircraft began to descend, for a few moments he allowed the exotic appeal of the name *Singapore* to revolve in his mind. All his life the idea of distant travel had appealed to him. Now he was doing it, and a certain sense of adventure stirred within him. He couldn't help it; it was part of his being.

The landing was smooth and seemingly effortless. When he stepped out of the jetway, he found himself in a very large, immaculately clean terminal. As he walked with his fellow passengers toward immigration and customs, he was impressed by the size of the facility and its efficient design. Everything about it suggested that it was brand-new.

At one of the many immigration booths, he noted with professional interest that his name was run through a computer before he was handed back his passport and was told, "Welcome to Singapore." It all took only a few seconds, so the system obviously was up to date.

As he started toward the baggage claim area, he was intercepted. The man who halted him was at least six feet four. He was immaculate in a smart uniform topped off by a dark green, tightly wound turban. His appearance was completed by an impressive full beard. "Good afternoon, sir," he said with only a hint of an accent. "Are you Mr. Tibbs?"

"Yes, I'm Virgil Tibbs."

"Superintendent Lee's compliments, sir. He had every intention of meeting you himself, but we had an unusually bad homicide early this morning and he is fully engaged. I am Inspector Ajit Singh from the Organized Crime Division." The tall man held out his hand.

As Tibbs took it, he noted the formal style of speech the

41

inspector used. It suggested that he had learned his English as a second or even a third language, but he had done so with precision.

"I'm pleased to meet you, Inspector," Tibbs said. "I've never been here before."

"So we understand, Mr. Tibbs. If I may have your stubs, your bags will be picked up. I have a car waiting."

"You're going to too much trouble for me," Tibbs said.

"Certainly not," the tall Sikh replied. "Especially in view of your injury. We know about that, of course. Being shot in the line of duty is not something any of us like to contemplate."

Singh's impressive stature, and his uniform, cleared a way past customs and through the main outer hall to where lines of taxis and busses were waiting. Within seconds a blue car marked POLICE slid up to the curb. "Your bags will be here shortly," Singh said. "Then we can go directly to your hotel."

Tibbs looked around him, taking it all in. The area was swarming with people. Most appeared to be Chinese. He saw some faces as dark as his own, but knew immediately that they were from a different segment of humanity. There were a few women in saris and some men in what appeared to be Malay dress. Others wore white Philippine shirts hanging outside their trousers. He heard a cacophony of language he could not comprehend, but the warmth of the tropical air spoke to him in a universal tongue. There was not a scrap of litter to be seen.

A porter hurried up with Tibbs's two bags, loaded them into the back of the police car, and then disappeared. No money appeared to change hands. "Please get in," Singh said.

Tibbs climbed in the back. Despite the small size of the car, there was ample room. Singh, who was a much bigger man, fit himself in without trouble, despite the tall turban on his head.

"You said that you were from the Organized Crime Division," Tibbs said. "I had no idea that the Mafia had penetrated to this part of the world."

"Our organized crime is not the same as yours," Singh responded. "Our section deals principally with the secret societies. Where there are Chinese, there will be secret societies. It is a cultural thing. Keeping them under control requires constant attention."

When the car started up, it was quiet for a minute. Driving on the left was unfamiliar to Tibbs, but fortunately it was not his responsibility.

"You mentioned that you had a particularly bad homicide this morning," he said. "Can you tell me what happened?"

"On a confidential basis, yes, since you are our guest. If you will look to your right, you will see some high rises. There are many of these in Singapore, and we are putting up more. We have more than two million people here, and all of them are being decently housed.

"In one of these high rises an apartment was occupied by a family of six: mother and father with two sons and two daughters. The mother awoke in the night and went to see her children. She found one of the little girls brutally murdered."

Although he was in a totally strange place, a sense of involvement arose in Tibbs; he could not help it.

"Was the door locked?"

"Yes."

"Any evidence of an intruder?"

"None."

"On what floor is the apartment?"

"The seventh."

"The means of murder?"

"A sharp knife. It may have been taken from the kitchen. The mother is too distraught to be questioned properly."

Tibbs sat back in his seat. "I see what you mean. Even

43

though it's a walk-through, the death of a child makes it very bad."

Singh showed an increased interest. "I am not familiar with that American expression; what is a 'walk-through'?"

"It's a case, Inspector, where the culprit is obvious at once. Often he is anxious to confess. But under our system all of the evidence has to be gathered just the same, all of the statements taken, all the interviews conducted, and an airtight case built for presentation in court."

"I see, Mr. Tibbs, but this is not a walk-through, for one particular reason. The murder weapon has not been recovered."

Tibbs took a moment to look out at the panorama of palm trees, multiple high-rise housing structures, the edge of the South China Sea, and the obviously very new freeway on which they were driving.

"Have you had time for a thorough search?" he asked.

"Since the crime was discovered in the early hours of the morning, yes. The apartment is quite small, and it has been gone over three times. The knife is not there."

Tibbs sat up a little straighter once more. "There are windows, of course."

"Certainly. The ground for a wide radius was carefully searched. There was no knife and no evidence of any blood. We don't know for sure that the knife was bloodied, but it is likely."

"Then someone must have picked it up. I could name certain parts of some American cities, Inspector, where a knife thrown out like that would hardly hit the ground. Even at that hour of the night."

"Mr. Tibbs, in that area there is some foot traffic at all hours. And most of the residents are Chinese, which means that nothing whatever would go unnoticed."

"I see." Tibbs took a moment before he asked, "Is there any kind of a roadway close by?"

Singh turned to face Tibbs more fully. "Yes, at a short distance. A capable man could have thrown the knife that far. However, there is a police post only a few yards away. I don't believe that the knife could have landed on the roadway."

"If you will allow me, Inspector, I was thinking of a case that happened not long ago in Los Angeles County. A gun was thrown out of a window into the back of a passing garbage truck."

Singh sat still for a second or two. "I don't know if that was checked," he said. "It will be difficult, but we should look into it. Driver, hand me the microphone."

While Singh was talking, Tibbs noted that they were approaching the downtown area. Very tall buildings, many of them of distinctive architecture, thrust up toward the sky. Shops began to proliferate, traffic had increased, and there were steady streams of pedestrians on both sides of the street. This was indeed Singapore, but if Tibbs had had any visions of native girls in sarongs leaning languidly against inviting palm trees, the modern metropolis that surrounded him dispelled them without mercy.

Singh interrupted his thoughts. "We will look into it; thank you for the suggestion. Meanwhile, we are approaching Orchard Road, which is the Broadway, or the Wilshire Boulevard, of Singapore. You will find the Crossroads Hotel excellent, I'm sure. Since you may wish to conduct interviews, a suite has been arranged for you."

"Thank you," Tibbs said. "Will it be the same one that was occupied by Mrs. Motamboru?"

Singh gave a half smile. "Yes, that is correct. Please sign for all of your meals and necessary services. Your bill has been arranged."

The pain in Tibbs's side had been intensified by the drive in, and he was anxious for it to be over.

The police car turned and entered the wide driveway of

what was obviously a top quality hotel. As the driver pulled up before the entranceway and stopped, a splendidly costumed doorman came forward and let Tibbs out. Singh got out on his own from the other side. While the luggage was being unloaded, he drew Tibbs away a few steps where he could speak without being overheard.

"Mr. Tibbs," he said, "we are, of course, aware that Madam Motamboru is a person of importance. We are concerned with our case, yes, but we are more concerned with the truth. If you can prove her innocent, you will have our sincere thanks."

"Thank you," Tibbs said.

"I'll leave you now to rest after your journey. Later a representative of the police will contact you here. Meanwhile, please call me if there is anything at all that I can do for you."

"I'm most grateful, Inspector Singh" was the best that Tibbs could manage.

The tall Sikh straightened himself even more for a moment and then slightly changed the tone of his voice. "I only wish," he said, and then paused, "that the task you are undertaking were not so difficult. When you have rested, we will explain to you that she has told us an impossible story, one that cannot possibly be believed. If you can persuade her to be more truthful with us, then we may be able to do something to help her. I speak as one policeman to another."

"Thank you, Inspector," Tibbs said. "I can only say to you that I will do the best that I am able."

Chapter Six

When Virgil Tibbs saw the suite that had been assigned to him, he had a sharp reaction that this was how the other half lived. It was more than spacious and comfortable; it was almost the epitome of luxury. There was one large white sofa that looked so soft and inviting he had to give it an immediate try. When he sat down, he sank in so deeply he was almost buried in soft down. His early boyhood flashed back into his mind, reminding him of the worn-out, badly scarred furniture that had been part of his first home. He got back to his feet and resolved to snap out of it.

He knew he had been given this elegant suite so that he could make a detailed examination of the place where the killing had occurred without having to disturb anyone.

After spending a few minutes looking down at Orchard Road, one of the shopping meccas of the world, he unpacked and hung up his clothes. He longed for a comfortable shower to relax his body from the strains of travel, but his dressings made that impossible. The jet lag he was experiencing insisted it was the small hours of the morning. Without any sense of guilt he climbed into a wonderfully comfortable bed and was asleep in moments.

Assistant Superintendent Lee Kong Ho received word that his friend had arrived at a time when he was extremely busy. He had just finished an extended second interview of Tan Khin Peow, the father of the slain child and the only visible suspect.

The fact that Tan's background was impeccable was significant, but it was by no means a guarantee of his innocence. There were few people indeed, Lee knew, who did not have private secrets of some kind locked in their hearts. Yet the interview had only strengthened Tan's story that he had known and heard nothing until his wife's screams had awakened him. His grief could not have been faked; Lee was certain of that. The tears that had rolled down Tan's cheeks had been real, and every other indication had been consistent with an innocent and cruelly bereaved father. Lee had not been able to dig up a single thing that was even remotely incriminating. There was no basis whatever to file charges against him.

The Scene of the Crime Unit had done its work well; the apartment had been gone over in meticulous detail. There were dust samples still to be analyzed, and vacuumings from the floor to be examined, but the preliminary report was that no evidence whatever had been turned up, other than the body itself and the liberal amount of blood that had been spilled. The murder weapon had still not been recovered.

Inquiries were also being made concerning any open-bodied trucks that might have passed by the murder scene during the critical time. It was accepted that these inquiries probably would be fruitless, but they were carried out nonetheless.

Madam Wee, the mother of the victim, had been given a sedative by her doctor and ordered to rest. He strongly advised that questioning her be put off as long as possible. She and the three surviving children were being cared for at an undisclosed location. Outside the police post a crowd of the curious still clustered in the hope of catching some scrap of information or a glimpse of a principal officer on the case. Gossip ran rampant, flowing backward and forward like a tide.

Superintendent Pandian Subramaniam, who headed the Homicide Division, had come by twice. He left each time satisfied that Lee was doing his job and would not benefit from any higher level interference.

When the day was drawing to a close and the investigation was already a good twelve hours old, Lee finally called it quits for the moment. There was simply nothing more to be done at the murder scene. He conferred with Inspector Fong, who was in command of the afternoon shift at the Khe Bong Police Post, and then released the premises back to its usual occupants.

It would be no pleasure for Tan and his family to return to their home, but that problem they would have to deal with themselves. Lee felt a genuine compassion for them, but his main attention was focused on finding the person who had been responsible for such an utterly heartless crime. The best hope he had was that the lab reports would contain somethings useful. Few criminals knew what a good crime lab could do, or how tiny grains of evidence could often be magnified into a capital conviction.

Before going home to rest, Lee called first on Superintendent Subramaniam to give his superior a verbal report. As soon as he was in the office, the superintendent called the commissary for tea, which arrived almost at once. "If you had any good news, you would have already told me," he said as the hot beverage was served.

"Correct, sir," Lee agreed. "As of this moment I have nothing to go on—nothing at all."

The superintendent, whose dark complexion showed his Indian origins, was thoughtful as he sipped his tea. "Could the father be guilty?" he asked.

"I very much doubt it," Lee replied. "Not just because of his good record. There's no motive. Also the man is genuinely grief stricken."

49

"I had in mind a possible motive," Subramaniam said. "There are four children and they're pretty close in age. It was the youngest who was killed, wasn't it?"

"Correct, sir, and I see your point: she might have been one too many. I thought of that myself, but the grief of the parents was so genuine, I discarded that theory. Also the father has a very comfortable income, more than enough to care for a family of six."

"Then we are left with two possibilities: the mother, which I tend to doubt, or an intruder. Were any special locks fitted to the door?"

"No, just the usual kind. Anyone with the proper picks could open it in seconds. Madam Wee, Tan's wife, required medical attention. I had a word with the doctor after he saw her. It was his professional opinion that for her to have killed her own child was out of the question."

"There is nothing yet, I take it, on the murder weapon."

"No, sir, not yet."

The superintendent drank a little more tea. "We're going to need a break, I think."

"Definitely." Lee was a little tense as he reached for his own tea. "I can't recall a case where there has been such a blank wall. The Scene of the Crime people came up empty except for lab material. I have no motive, no murder weapon, no evidence whatever that I can use."

The superintendent allowed himself a grim smile. "Then perhaps it is fortunate that your friend Mr. Virgil Tibbs is in town," he said.

Inspector Ajit Singh, meanwhile, supplied a brief verbal report directly to the deputy commissioner. "Tibbs is a gentleman," he said. "I was very relieved to discover that. I could see evidence of his injury in the way he walked, but he did not speak of it. He is not the kind of man to raise his voice or make unwanted waves."

"For this blessing, Buddha be praised."

"One point, sir," Singh continued. "I had mentioned the Tan killing to him and he inquired about it, as a matter of professional interest. When I told him that the murder weapon had not been recovered, he cited a similar case in which a gun had been tossed into the back of a passing garbage truck."

Sim leaned back in his chair. "That's a thought," he conceded.

"I agree, sir, and inquiries are being made. Perhaps there was indeed such a case. It is also possible that Tibbs was being exceptionally tactful in offering a suggestion."

"Perhaps," Sim said thoughtfully, "he may be a little more difficult to dispose of than we thought."

Tibbs awoke sometime in the middle of the night. It was still far too early to be up and about, so he picked up a book he had brought with him and settled down to read. When the room began to grow lighter, he put down his book, went to the window, and watched as the tropical dawn brought swiftly rising flame to the sky.

God willing, he thought, in this new day he would be able to see Miriam again.

He took a careful stand-up bath to keep his dressings dry. After shaving he dressed in a pair of cream slacks and a light blue sports coat that helped to mask the inevitable bulges that the dressings produced.

It was then he noticed that a note had been pushed under his door. He picked it up and read the few lines carefully written in a precise hand:

Mr. Virgil Tibbs:
When you are ready for your breakfast, I would be pleased if you would join me. I shall be waiting in the lobby.

> *Osman Bin Mohamed*
> *Superintendent of Police*

51

Virgil picked up a telephone and pushed the button for the front desk. "This is Mr. Tibbs," he said. "I believe a gentleman is waiting for me, a Mr. Osman Bin Mohamed. I hope I pronounced that correctly."

"Yes, sir, you did. Superintendent Mohamed is here. Do you wish to speak with him?"

"No, but please tell him that I'll be right down."

"I will inform him. Thank you, sir."

Virgil checked that he had his wallet, his I.D.s, and an ample supply of traveler's checks; then he went to meet his new police contact.

When he stepped off the elevator into the huge and dramatic lobby, he was faced by another mix of peoples from many parts of the world. A tourist bus was discharging its contents, and a crowd of obvious Americans was gathering around the reception desk. As Tibbs approached the desk himself, he heard someone say behind him, "I didn't know they had any blacks in Singapore."

"They're everywhere," a male voice rumbled in response, in a thick and heavy accent.

At that moment Tibbs was touched on the arm. He turned to find himself facing a pleasant-looking, very slender man casually dressed in a light tan safari suit. He had dark, alert eyes and jet-black hair that set off his slightly narrow features. By appearance he was thirty-five at the most. "Virgil Tibbs," he said, making it a statement.

"Yes."

"Osman Mohamed. I got your message. I hope you haven't eaten yet." His English was casual and flawless; by intonation it was western American.

"No, I haven't."

"Then let's go."

The superintendent led the way to a quite elegant coffee shop where breakfast was being served. The hostess nodded in recognition and seated them in an isolated booth well removed from her other customers.

"You have a choice of breakfasts," the superintendent said. "Chinese, Malay, Indonesian, Indian, continental, or American. The Indonesian is pretty hot if you're not used to it."

"Just for this morning I'd better stick to what I know," Tibbs said. "Something like ordinary ham and eggs."

The young man closed his menu. "Fine, me too. But no ham." He raised his hand, which caused a very pretty Chinese waitress to materialize within seconds. When he had given the order, he took a second to adjust the silverware before him, then he looked up. "Kong Lee may join us if he can get away," he said. "He's looking forward to seeing you again."

"That's certainly mutual," Tibbs replied.

"He's got a very tough case right now, a child homicide."

"I heard about it, Superintendent."

"Forget the title: Osman is fine. I'm in charge of the Prosecutions Division. In Singapore we don't go through a district attorney's office; we do our own filing and prosecute our own cases in court. Except for murder; those cases are conducted by the A.G.'s chambers. In this instance, I'm working with them."

"You don't know how many headaches you avoid."

"Perhaps we do. Now about Madam Motamboru. You understand that this is a very sensitive matter."

"Yes, of course." Tibbs was careful; the open manner of the superintendent did not deceive him.

He was interrupted by the waitress, who brought coffee and some inviting sweet buns to get them started.

As soon as she had left, the superintendent continued. "We know her reputation; she's a very accomplished lady. Her late husband was a good friend of our Prime Minister."

Tibbs reacted to that. "I didn't know that President Motamboru had close contacts with Singapore."

53

The youthful superintendent became more serious. "Singapore, Virgil, is at one of the most strategic spots on the globe. The Straits of Malacca are just west of us, which helps to make our harbor the second busiest anywhere. We are the crossroads for this part of the world; much of the commerce between Europe and the Far East clears through here. Without getting into geopolitics, it's common knowledge that some very ruthless forces are looking for any excuse to move in on top of us."

He remained silent, then, until the waitress reappeared with their breakfast orders. She served the food, poured more coffee, and made sure that everything was satisfactory before she withdrew.

"Now," Osman said. "I have to lay down some ground rules for you, which is why I'm here. We said we'd cooperate and we will, but there have to be some restrictions."

"What are they?" Tibbs asked.

"First of all, you won't be allowed to ride in any of our patrol units. Also, we can't permit you to visit any crime scenes."

Tibbs was normally unflappable, but that abrupt piece of news did not sit well at all. "That isn't the kind of cooperation we extend," he said. "We gave Inspector Lee the run of the place."

"I know you did," Osman answered. "And it was much appreciated. Let me explain. Depositions aren't accepted here. If you rode in a patrol car and witnessed an incident that ended up in court, you'd have to come back to Singapore, at government expense, to testify. You have to be here in person to be cross-examined. The same goes for crime scenes. So you can't be in on any of the action."

Virgil changed the topic. "Suppose that somehow I manage to prove Mrs. Motamboru innocent, what then?"

Osman finished a mouthful of food before he answered. "Officially, nothing. Off the record, they'd probably give you the Order of the Lotus Petal, second class, and make you an honorary citizen. The Prime Minster would be most grateful. But it's got to be airtight; a plea of amnesia or anything like that won't work."

At that moment a hand fell on Tibbs's shoulder; he looked up to see his friend Inspector, now Assistant Superintendent, Lee beside him. He got up quickly to shake hands. "Welcome to Singapore," Lee said, "and thanks for the idea about the open truck. It could pan out yet." He seated himself and signaled the waitress for coffee. "Any more bright ideas, Virgil?"

Tibbs hesitated. "One did hit me this morning although it's none of my business."

"Make it your business," Lee invited as the waitress filled his cup.

"On the way in from the airport I noticed that in most of the housing developments people had stuck their laundry out on poles from their windows."

"True. It's done all over the city. We call it the flag of Singapore."

"Are the poles bamboo?"

"Yes."

"Then they're hollow," Tibbs said.

Lee gave him a professionally pleasant smile. "Thanks, Virgil. We thought of that, but if you get any more good ideas, pass them on. Meanwhile, I came by to apologize that I can't be with you until this one is cleared up. Watch out for Osman here. He's our sharpest legal eagle. That's why he's come up so fast."

"I already got the message," Tibbs responded.

Lee quickly finished his coffee and then stood up. "See you later," he said, and hurried out of the room.

Mohamed was deceptively calm. "When you've finished your breakfast," he said. "You have an appointment. I've set up a time for you to see Madam Motamboru."

A quick current ran down Tibbs's spine, but he kept his voice calm. "Perhaps I ought to contact the embassy first."

"You're expected there at two this afternoon."

Tibbs touched his lips with his napkin. "Then I'm ready now," he said.

Chapter Seven

Osman had a plain blue unmarked police car with a driver waiting for him outside the hotel. While Tibbs climbed in back, the youthful superintendent joined him from the other side.

As the car slipped into the traffic stream on Orchard Road, Virgil turned to his companion. "Do you mind a personal question?" he asked.

"Go right ahead."

"How did you manage to achieve so much rank so quickly?"

"First of all, Virgil, I had the educational qualifications. A college graduate enters the police department at a higher level than other applicants, particularly if he has fluent language capability. I came in as an inspector because I had my law degree, a doctorate actually, and some other qualifications. Without them I would have started as a constable."

"I see."

"Of course I still had to go through a period of intensive training before I could assume my duties in the Prosecutions Division."

After some minutes Tibbs saw that they had left Orchard Road for a much quieter, winding street. As seemed to be true of Singapore everywhere, it was well paved, without potholes, and totally free of litter. The car rolled among smoothly, the driver apparently paying no attention whatever to the conversation taking place behind him.

More high-rise housing projects appeared with others under construction. In every direction T-shaped cranes marked the landscape.

After some minutes the car turned into a driveway and pulled up before a manned gate. The driver spoke to the police guard on duty, then Osman produced an I.D. It was obvious that the guard knew him, but the formality of proper identification was still observed. Seconds later the gate was opened and the car drove in.

As they walked toward the entrance doorway, Osman had a final word. "This is the women's prison. You understand why we have to keep Madam Motamboru here like any other female awaiting trial. She's being cared for reasonably well, but we can't afford to be caught playing favorites."

"Will I be allowed to speak with her privately?" Tibbs asked.

"Absolutely. You can have as much time as you like, and you have my word that you won't be watched or overheard. All I ask is that you don't give her anything, or talk about your interview afterward to the press."

"I'm not about to hang myself," Tibbs said.

"Good. What happened in her country is officially none of our business, but we're not blind to the situation there. Now I've got to get back, but there'll be a car and driver for you when you're ready. You know about your appointment at the American embassy."

Tibbs raised his right hand to express his thanks. He knew that Muslims had some taboo about shaking hands, but at that moment it eluded him. Osman returned his gesture and then turned away.

Inside the front door there was a reception counter where Tibbs found that he was expected. After a brief delay, an orderly dressed in a crisp tan uniform showed him into a very plain room equipped with a metal table and four institutional chairs. There was a large barred window that admitted a generous amount of supportive daylight. Some of the panels were open to admit fresh air and a hint of bird songs from the outside.

He had been in the room for about three minutes when the door opened once more. A female officer in uniform appeared and ushered in Miriam Motamboru. Then she closed the door and left them alone.

Tibbs stood very still, looking at the woman who had made such a change in his life. She had on a plain blue jail dress, vastly different from the designer clothes he was accustomed to seeing her wear. Her hair was very simply combed, and she wore no cosmetics at all. With her hands clasped in front of her, she stood perfectly still, waiting for him to make the first move.

He walked toward her and held out his hands part way, giving her the option. Miriam came almost hesitantly to meet him, then without warning he was holding her in his arms, feeling the warmth of her body against his own. The intervening months, and the reason for their meeting, vanished into oblivion; he only cared that he was with her once again—the wonderfully compelling person who, despite his determined self control, had so completely captivated him not too long ago.

After a few moments she pulled away, but held on to his hands. She looked at him and swallowed hard. "Thank you for coming," she said.

Tibbs gave her hands a slight squeeze and then let them go. "I was glad to," he responded.

Miriam seated herself on one of the straight, hard chairs, keeping her eyes on his face. He sat down opposite her, took a deep breath, and asked, "How are you?"

"I'm as well as I could ask, under the circumstances."

"And the children?"

"They're safe, thank God, in Switzerland. They're being protected there. It's them I'm concerned about now. I need to be free to look after them."

"Of course," he said.

Tears began to appear on her face. "Virgil, he was such a good man! All he did was help his people. He was wonderful, and he died so horribly. *Why, Virgil, why?*"

He tried to frame an answer for her, but he could not put one into words. He watched while she produced a plain handkerchief and wiped her eyes. Then she gathered herself together and forced her mind into another channel. "Virgil, I never killed anyone!"

He tried to put strength and comfort into his voice. "I know that, Miriam, that's why I'm here. To help if I can. But so far I've got nothing to go on. So you'll have to help me. No matter how hard it may be for you, I want to take you through *everything* that has happened. Start at the very beginning and don't leave even the smallest thing out."

Quietly Miriam began to compose herself. "After I was arrested," she said, "I asked to see the American ambassador. I told him that much more was at stake than my own welfare. I also told him that I needed someone I could completely trust. I gave him your name. I think for the sake of my husband the Singapore authorities have been very considerate, although I know they don't believe what I told them. They even arranged for you to stay in my suite, so that you could examine it if you need to."

She looked at him and then drew a sharp breath. "Virgil, what's happened to you?" She touched his side where the bulge of the dressings was visible.

"I was shot during an attempted robbery," he answered. "It could have been much worse. I'm recovering well."

60

Miriam reached her arm halfway across the table. "Virgil, what kind of world are we living in?"

"Never mind that now," he said. "I want to hear everything you can tell me."

Miriam looked about her at the very plain room. As she did, Tibbs read what was on her mind. "We're alone," he assured her. "A man I respect told me we wouldn't be listened to or observed. Now, please, tell me everything. Don't leave out even the least detail." He folded his hands and then squeezed them so hard his dark fingers were visibly paler. His concentration was total.

"I have to begin with my husband," Miriam said. She spoke slowly, choosing her words very carefully. "He had an excellent education and was a very good administrator. After the ruling council chose him as President, he worked hard to bring democracy to Bakara, even though many parts of our country are still occupied by primitive tribesmen. He encouraged development. Corruption had been a way of life for generations; he began a program to root it out." She paused and wiped her eyes. "He was a very wonderful man."

"*Newsweek* called him the most enlightened leader in black Africa."

Miriam clasped her hands together. "Virgil, he *was!* That's why he was killed. The countries around us were filled with Russians. Cuban troops were shipped in to do the fighting. We were infiltrated by hordes of communist organizers. You see, we have mineral deposits everyone wanted. When they couldn't corrupt my husband, or any of his people, they used Muslim fanatics to start a holy war."

Miriam stopped and made a fresh effort to collect herself. When she continued, her voice was almost dangerously calm. "They managed to kill him, but there was something they didn't know. He kept careful records of everything that was going on: the attempts at bribery, the deceit, the things that the communists were doing. You weren't there, Virgil, so you can't imagine what it was like."

"Perhaps I can," he said. "A policeman sees a great many things. What happened to the records your husband kept?"

"They found out about them. I don't know how. But if they were made public, it would expose the whole communist effort in our part of the world. Everybody knows about Afghanistan and Grenada, but Africa . . ."

She brushed her hair back and composed herself once more. Tibbs knew what he was doing to her, but he had to hear her story first hand, every bit of it, before he could begin to help her. Obviously she knew that too.

"When things were becoming very dangerous, after I came back from Pasadena, my husband insisted that we send our children to a safe place. We settled on Switzerland, where we could put them in a good school. Then he wanted me to go away too, but I refused. Virgil, I don't think I can go on." She was in tears once more.

Tibbs moved his chair beside hers. Then he sat down and put his arm across her shoulders, letting his strength flow into her, giving her a sense of support and understanding. When she turned her tear-stained face toward him he took out a fresh handkerchief and carefully dried her eyes. Her fingers tightened as she clung to him.

"After . . . his death . . . some of the people he had trusted most kept me under protection. They elected me a member of the council. For his sake, I tried to do all that I could. It went on that way until our intelligence people were alerted by the Mossad to get me out of the country. We had an emergency council meeting. It was decided that I should leave at once, and take my husband's records with me. They had been reduced to microfilm, so they would be easy to carry. Is this all clear so far?"

Virgil nodded. "Just keep on the same way."

"The next morning I went to the airport under guard and took a flight to Geneva. When I arrived there, I was met by a man from the American embassy who put me on a plane to Zurich. He had made a reservation for me at a first-class hotel. They knew who I was, but I registered under an assumed name."

"And your husband's records?"

"I put them in the vault; it was the first thing I did. Virgil, there are people who would give almost anything to see them destroyed. As you say in America, it could blow them right out of the water." She managed a momentary smile. "I heard you use that expression once."

"What did you do after that?" Tibbs prompted.

"The next morning the same official came to see me. I asked to meet with the American ambassador as soon as possible. He told me that the ambassador was out of the country and would be gone for two weeks. The council had instructed me to give my husband's records to the ambassador personally, at the embassy. I was warned to be very careful because our opposition was utterly ruthless. They didn't have to tell me that."

For a moment it appeared she would not be able to continue, but she did.

"The American official and I had breakfast together in my room. He told me that he did not think it advisable for me to wait the full two weeks for the ambassador to return."

"Did he ask you why you wanted to see him?"

"Yes. I told him that I had a message from our ruling council to your President that I was to deliver personally to the ambassador. He accepted that. He explained that the Swiss are very touchy about their neutrality; of course I already knew that. He told me I was requested to go on to Singapore, where special arrangements were being made. He told me that an American agent would contact me on the way for my protection, and how he would identify himself. Then he took my passport to get the necessary visa. It was returned that afternoon with the visa and a round-trip ticket. I expected to be back within a few days."

"Wouldn't it have been simpler, since the film was in a safe place, to wait for the ambassador to return?"

"That was my thought, Virgil, but the American agent told me that for certain reasons time was very important. I had already received a message from Bakara, asking me to come home. Because of the short time since I had left, I thought it might be unwise. So I agreed to come to Singapore."

"What name did the American agent give you?"

"Mr. Robertson. His first name was Willis: I saw it when he showed me his I.D."

"How did this second agent contact you?"

"He didn't. He was to have joined me on the plane at Bangkok, but he didn't appear."

"Were you given a back-up plan?"

"No, so I came on to Singapore and checked into the Crossroads Hotel, where I had a reservation."

"Were you contacted there?"

"Yes. I had a call from the American embassy here. I was asked to stay where I was and told I would be called again shortly."

"Did you know the person who called you?"

"No, but I rang the embassy back at the listed number and asked to speak to the person who had just called me. She came on the line and verified her identity."

"I'll look into that," Tibbs said. He took out a notebook and made an entry. "Now, the next part is vital. Be sure you give me every possible detail you can remember."

Miriam squared her shoulders, "Virgil, a long time ago I learned to shoot. I never went hunting, I couldn't, but ever since I was kidnapped, you remember that, I've had an international permit to carry a gun. Our diplomatic service arranged it. I never used it until I left home this last time. Then I took a gun with me."

"That was probably prudent," Tibbs said. "As long as you knew how to use it."

"I do. So I was armed when I came to Singapore."

"The local authorities knew this?"

"Yes. I had called our diplomatic people in Europe to tell them where I was going; they notified the police. I was met at the airport and driven to the Crossroads. I had been preregistered, so I was shown directly up to the suite."

"Nothing else happened during your arrival here?"

"No, nothing at all. Virgil, do you need the details of everything that I did after that?"

"Every scrap. If you stopped to sneeze in the lobby, tell me about it."

For a moment Miriam just looked at him; in that brief fraction of time he sensed that she was confiding completely in him. It gave his confidence a little added strength, but it also underlined his heavy responsibility.

"I was tired when I arrived," Miriam continued, "so I just stayed in my room. When it was time, I had dinner sent up and I ate alone."

"Can you describe the waiter who brought it?"

"Actually two men came, a waiter in uniform and a hotel official in a very well-cut, dark business suit. The waiter was Chinese and about thirty. The other man was there to see if I needed anything else."

"Probably security," Tibbs said, more to himself than to her. "What did you have?"

"Lamb chops. They were excellent."

For a moment Tibbs relaxed and smiled. "That's the ultimate compliment," he said. "One of the first things you told me was that you were a very good cook. You certainly are."

Miriam used both of her hands to hold his. "I hope I can cook for you again—soon," she said.

"Anything else that day?"

"No, nothing: not even any phone calls. The maid came in to turn down the bed. She left a piece of chocolate on the pillow and several more on a table. I read for a little while and then went to sleep."

"The next day?"

Miriam drew her hands back and folded them in her lap. "In the morning, breakfast was brought to my room. Again there were two men: a waiter and an assistant manager. I know because he gave me his card."

"You kept it?"

"Yes. As soon as I was finished I went down to see the manager, Mr. Henderson Chang. I told him in confidence that I had something unusually important to deposit for safekeeping. He very discreetly asked what it was. I told him it was a document."

"Did you tell him it was film?"

"No. When he asked for it, I gave it to him; it was a small package. I had wrapped the film myself so that no outlines would show through. I sealed it before I left home; it was still unopened. Mr. Chang wrote me a receipt for it, then he took it with him and left the room. When he returned, he handed me a key. I remember exactly what he said. 'Our vault is very secure; you can depend on it. If anyone other than you presents this key, our security people will be alerted immediately.' "

"Do you still have the key?" Tibbs asked.

"No," Miriam answered. "When I was arrested, I had the key with me. My handbag was searched and the key was found. I was interviewed by a Superintendent Lee. When he asked me to identify the key, of course I did."

"Did he ask what you had put in the deposit box?"

"Yes. I told him it was a document intended for your President. He asked me if he could open the box in the presence of the American ambassador. I agreed to that, if I could speak to the ambassador first."

"Did you?"

"Yes. I was allowed to call the American embassy. The ambassador assured me that a judge would also be present when the box was opened."

Tibbs face became very grave. "So the police have the microfilm," he said.

Miriam seemed to flinch under his steady look. "No, Virgil. They swore to me that when they opened the box, they found that it was empty."

Chapter Eight

Virgil Tibbs shut his eyes, concentrating completely for a few seconds. Miriam waited anxiously until he was ready to continue.

"Now comes the most important part," he said. "So far you've given me a good account, although I have a lot more questions to ask later. Now, was this the day of the shooting?" He made no effort to use a euphemism; it was not the time for such niceties.

"Yes."

"What did you do after breakfast?"

"I went out for a little while. I had only been in Singapore once before, and I wanted to get the feel of the city."

"Did you consider that safe?"

"Why not? The film I had been carrying was secure in the vault, at least I thought that it was. I had no reason to worry, and Orchard Road was already full of people."

"Did you have any particular destination in mind?"

"Yes, an Oriental art shop where my husband had chosen some things." She stopped and shook her head. "That may have been foolish, because if I bought anything I wasn't sure I would have a home to put it in. But I went there anyway."

"What is the shop?"

"The Moongate."

"Did you make a purchase?"

"Yes, a jade pendant."

"Where is it now?"

"I don't know. It was among my things. The hotel must have them somewhere."

"When did you return to the hotel?"

"At ten minutes to one. I remember looking at the clock as I came through the lobby."

"Were there any other incidents, of any kind, while you were out?"

"No, nothing. A few people stared at me, but I'm used to that."

"Were there any messages for you when you returned?"

"Yes, one. It said, 'You can expect a visitor at three this afternoon.' "

"Any signature?"

"No. It came over the phone."

"Then what did you do?"

"I went up to my room. I washed for lunch and called for a reservation at the French restaurant in the hotel. They told me I could come right down. The maitre d' showed me to a private table that was partially screened from the rest of the room. I had a very good light lunch: poached salmon, with a custard for dessert. Then I went back to my suite."

"What time was it then?"

"Close to two. The service was very good in the restaurant, but it took time to prepare my food."

"You had an hour, then, before your visitor was expected."

"Yes, almost exactly."

Tibbs made some more notes. "Were you going to admit your visitor without knowing who he was?" he asked.

Miriam rested her forearms in the table. "I'd better explain, Virgil, that when a head of state travels, or his wife, special precautions are always taken. Phone calls are carefully screened. Any visitors are cleared first, and then shown up by a member of the security staff. My room number is never given out; deliveries from the outside are taken over by security and delivered by someone on the hotel staff."

"What did you think when you got the message?"

"I was expecting an American representative, since I had called the embassy."

"Did your visitor come promptly?"

"Yes, almost to the minute."

"Give me a description."

"A man about forty-five or fifty, and very fit. He was about five feet ten by your measurements, and well built: a lot like you, Virgil. He had medium-blond hair, still quite full, cut almost in military style. He wore a very good light gray suit."

"He was a Caucasian, then."

"Yes. He spoke excellent English without a trace of an accent. I think most women would call him attractive."

"Was there anything special about his appearance?"

"No, his features weren't that distinctive. They were regular, that's all I can say."

"Color of eyes?"

"Brown, I think, but I can't be sure of that. I'm sorry, I should have noticed."

"What name did he give?"

"John Smith. He explained that many people really have that name."

"Exactly how did you receive him?"

"He was shown in by a hotel security man. He stayed with us until I told him he could go. I expected him to wait outside, but apparently he didn't."

Tibbs reacted to that. "How sure are you that he didn't stay?"

"If he had been there, Virgil, I wouldn't be in the mess I'm in now."

"It's customary for a security man to cover you that way?"

"Oh yes! Almost always there's at least one, sometimes two, when someone calls. Even someone I know."

"So you had every reason to believe that the man was there."

"Yes, I just said so."

"I know, but I want to impress that on your mind. Don't forget it for a minute. It could be important to your defense."

For the first time Miriam looked frightened. "Virgil, is this going to trial?"

"I hope not, but right now we can't overlook a single bet. Now tell me about Smith: what he said, what he did."

"As soon as I invited him to sit down, he apologized on behalf of the American government that I had not been contacted coming out of Bangkok. He told me there had been a potential security problem in Zurich and it had been thought best to get me out of there as soon as possible. Because of that, Singapore had been chosen as the place for me to meet with an American ambassador. I can see why: it's a beautiful city with wonderful accommodations, shopping—everything I might want."

"Did Mr. Smith mention any of this?"

"He referred to it."

"What did you think of him?"

"He was very well mannered. Virgil, am I helping you at all?"

"Yes," Tibbs answered. "So far there are six things that don't add up. I'm sure the police have spotted them, but I'll look into them further." He crossed his legs and laid his notebook on the table. "What happened next?" he asked.

"Mr. Smith said that the ambassador wanted to see me.

He asked if eleven the next morning would be convenient. I agreed to that if I could meet the ambassador at the embassy."

Tibbs nodded. "That was a sensible precaution, unless you happened to know the ambassador personally."

"No, I've never met him."

"Go on."

"Mr. Smith had a little trouble with a cough, so I got him a glass of water. He thanked me and took it. When I turned to take the empty glass away, I suddenly felt his arm across my throat."

Tibbs stood up. "Miriam, come here a moment," he said. When she complied, he turned her around so that her back was to him. "I'm going to do this very gently," he told her, "but I want you to tell me, if you can, if this is the grip he used." Tibbs put his left arm across her throat and locked it into position with his right. He applied no pressure at all, but Miriam could not have resisted. As soon he let her go, she turned back to him.

"Virgil, you frighten me sometimes! As far as I can tell, that's exactly what he did. Except that he pressed very hard."

"How long before you lost consciousness?"

Miriam's look appealed for understanding. "It wasn't long. I tried to cry out for the security man, but I couldn't make a sound."

"Where was your gun during this time?"

"In the drawer of the nightstand beside my bed. That's where I thought it best to keep it."

Tibbs made another note.

"When you came to, exactly what was the situation? Not what they told you, what *you yourself* saw."

"When I came to, I was lying on the floor of the living room. I had a pounding headache, so bad I was afraid to move. I heard a noise at the door, a knocking. First ordinary, then louder. I tried to get up, but I couldn't. The door opened and some people came in. That's all I can say— some people. I was helped to my feet, but I could barely stand."

Tibbs wrote again.

"I was helped into a chair, and I remember someone saying that the doctor should be called. I was sitting there, trying to recover myself, when I saw the man lying on the floor, about fifteen feet from where I had been. Then I saw my gun."

"Close to where you had been found?"

"Yes. Someone picked up the phone: I heard him ask for the doctor and the police."

"Did you see him make the call?"

"No, the phone was behind me. In a few moments Mr. Chang, the manager, came in. He gave some immediate orders. I remember a maid with a vacuum cleaner tried to come in and he sent her away. The doctor came very quickly; he was wearing a turban. He asked that I be taken into the bedroom. A young woman came with him; from the hotel staff, I believe."

"Did the doctor examine you?"

"Yes. I was still not myself, things were in a kind of haze. I do remember that he looked at my arms very carefully, and my legs. Then he sent someone for a prescription. By the time it came, the police were there. An officer helped me to sit up while I drank a glass of liquid the doctor gave me. As soon as I took it, I felt much better."

"Miriam," Tibbs said, "I want you to think very carefully. Did you feel any sort of itch, anything like that, on any part of your body?"

Miriam shook her head. "I don't think so."

Tibbs was very careful. "I don't want to put any ideas into your head," he said, "but there is one particular place where women have been given shots where the mark may not be found. All good pathologists know it."

Miriam clasped her hands together and shut her eyes to think. "Yes," she said. "Yes!" She looked at Virgil. "Under my left breast, just at the crease—"

He nodded.

"I remember now that my bra was uncomfortable. Is it too late . . . ?"

"Much too late," Tibbs said. "I presume the doctor didn't check there."

"No, he didn't."

"You had just taken the drink the doctor gave you," Tibbs prompted.

"Yes, and as I said, I felt much better. I got to my feet and went back into the living room. I remember that Mr. Chang was still there, the man who is head of hotel security, the doctor, and some policemen. Just after that Superintendent Lee arrived."

"Otherwise everything was just as it had been?"

"Yes."

"The gun on the floor."

"Yes."

"And Smith's body was where he had fallen."

"No, Virgil."

Tibbs looked surprised. "It had already been removed?" he asked.

"No, the body was still there. But that's the whole trouble, Virgil, that's why they won't believe me. It wasn't Mr. Smith. I told them that. I could see the face. I know it sounds impossible, but it was a different person altogether, a man I'd never seen before."

Chapter Nine

At the American embassy Tibbs found himself in the midst of a jumble of people lined up before a series of visa counters. On the right-hand side there was a window marked INQUIRIES; he presented himself there and handed over his card. It said Pasadena Police Department, but it was the only one he had. He was invited to sit down and wait.

He had only been seated briefly when a young woman came out to see him. She was moderately tall and dressed for the tropics in a white blouse and a powder-blue skirt. "Mr. Tibbs," she said in a voice that carried a twinge of Southern accent, "will you come in, please."

She led the way to a side door that opened into a different atmosphere altogether. The office she indicated was comfortably large and cool. Decoration was limited, but a beautifully carved Indonesian garuda almost five feet tall stood in one corner. "I'm sorry that the ambassador isn't here," the young woman said as she sat behind the desk. "I'm Janice Oliver. Would you prefer coffee or a cold drink?"

"Nothing, thank you."

"We're fully informed, of course, about your reason for being here and the credentials you're carrying. Could I see them please?"

Tibbs took out his wallet and passed over the basic I.D.

he had been issued. His hostess looked at it and then checked the photograph. "You also have another one, I understand."

"Yes, for emergencies." He didn't offer to produce it.

"You know, of course," the young woman continued, "about the close relationship we had with Mr. Motamboru and his government. His death was a great loss, to us as well as to Bakara."

"I never met him," Tibbs said, "but I completely agree, Miss Oliver."

His hostess glanced at her bare ring finger. "Thank you for not calling me 'Ms.,' " she said. "I'm very much for women's rights, but I dislike that label intensely. Getting back to the matter at hand, Mr. Tibbs, this is a very sensitive corner of the world. Any obvious favoritism shown to President Motamboru's widow could bring in a howling mob of professional agitators, even terrorists. Singapore has four major races, all with different religious faiths, living here in complete harmony. They very much want to keep it that way."

She paused a moment. "Your reputation as a detective is well known; Sidney Poitier saw to that. I know about the evidence against Miriam Motamboru, but I've met her and I can't see her as a murderess."

"Miss Oliver—" Tibbs began.

"Janice."

"Janice, I came here convinced that Miriam had to be innocent. I know how very respectable people have gone berserk and committed serious crimes, but I can't see her doing that."

"I agree," Janice said. "Do you think you can help her?"

"Yes," Virgil answered. "I talked with her at some length this morning. I am now looking at two alternatives. One is that she either deliberately lied to me, or else she is completely confused about what happened to her. I'm rejecting those premises."

"And the other alternative?" Janice asked.

"Assuming that she was truthful and accurate during our interview, I know for a fact that she's innocent of the murder. But it will take a lot of hard work to prove it."

"Can I help in any way?"

"Yes, very definitely. In fact I was about to ask for your cooperation. I have to go back over every step of Mrs. Motamboru's account and you can help me very much if you will."

"Then with the ambassador's approval, I'll do all that I can for you."

"I'm very grateful," Tibbs said.

"Also, Mr. Tibbs—"

"Virgil."

"Also, Virgil, there's the matter of the missing microfilm."

Tibbs allowed his manner to ease. "I don't think that will present too much of a problem," he said.

Virgil went to his room to freshen up after his visit to the embassy. That done, he phoned down and asked for an appointment to see the hotel doctor. He was told that Dr. Ling would be able to see him in ten minutes and to come right to the medical office.

As he rode down the elevator he recalled that the doctor who had attended Miriam in the hotel had worn a turban. That didn't suggest a Dr. Ling, but he would find out more when he arrived.

The medical office in the hotel was a full facility with X-ray and even the necessary equipment for minor surgical procedures. When Tibbs was admitted by the receptionist nurse, he found Dr. Ling to be a smooth-featured young woman who was entirely professional in her manner. "What is your problem, Mr. Tibbs?" she asked.

"I'm a police officer," he told her. "I was shot about ten days ago and have some dressings that need changing."

Dr. Ling expressed no surprise whatever. "Please strip down to your skivvies," she said, "and lie on the table. Take whatever position is most comfortable for you."

Beginning with his shoes, Virgil complied. He stretched out on the paper-covered table on his side and rested his head on his right arm. With cool and efficient hands Dr. Ling began to go over him in detail. She listened to his chest, explored his abdomen, and took his blood pressure. She had him sit up while she applied a stethoscope to his back. Then she checked his throat, ears, nose, and the pupils of his eyes. "Are you an internist?" he asked.

"Yes, in addition to general practice," Dr. Ling answered, and continued with her work. She made careful notes as she went along. When it came time to remove the old dressings, she was surprisingly gentle. He had expected considerable discomfort when the old adhesive was peeled off, but she did not subject him to that. She used a solvent of some kind that she wiped off as quickly as it had done its work. "I'm required to report this gunshot wound to the police here," she said, "although obviously it isn't recent. I see no evidence of infection; it's healing well."

"Thank you," Tibbs said.

"You missed probable death by less than three inches," the doctor added, "but fortunately no vital areas were penetrated. Remain still, please, while I apply some new dressings."

When she was half finished, Virgil ventured a question. "I believe a colleague of yours saw Mrs. Motamboru after she was attacked in her suite."

"Yes, Dr. Singh. I was off that day. What is your room number, Mr. Tibbs?"

"Twenty-two eighteen."

"Wasn't that Madam Motamboru's suite?"

"Yes. I'm conducting an investigation into her case. May

I ask how you recognized the room number so quickly?"

"I prefer not to answer that, Mr. Tibbs. If you wish to talk with Dr. Singh, he will be in this afternoon. You may get dressed now. Keep those dressings dry as much as you can. They should be changed again in another two days."

"Thank you, Doctor."

Dr. Ling did not even respond to that. She left the room with the same unbroken cool efficiency that characterized her professional manner.

In contrast, Mr. Henderson Chang, the general manager, was quite warm and cordial. Shortly after he asked for an interview, Tibbs was ushered into the presence of the man responsible for the whole intricate complex that was the Crossroads Hotel.

Chang came across his sizable office with his hand out in greeting. "Mr. Tibbs, I was hoping to meet you before you left. We're very pleased to have you staying with us."

For a brief moment Virgil wondered if the flawlessly well-dressed manager in his elegant office was being slightly patronizing, then he discarded the idea. "Thank you for seeing me, Mr. Chang," he said as he shook hands. "May I say that I'm most impressed with this hotel, in every respect."

"Very kind of you to say so, Mr. Tibbs. Now tell me what I can do for you."

"As you may know, sir," Virgil began, "I'm an American police officer."

Chang smiled slightly. "Rather I would say a renowned detective. We try to keep up to date here in Singapore."

Before he could say anything more, the door opened to admit a waiter pushing a trolley. He served coffee with quiet professionalism and then offered a tray of tempting pastries. "I can recommend the Sacher torte," Chang said. "We make it from the original Viennese recipe."

"Then I'll have some," Tibbs told him. "Despite my resolution not to overeat."

A slice of the rich chocolate torte was served to both men before the waiter positioned the cart next to Chang's desk and then withdrew. "Please continue," the manager invited.

"Mr. Chang, I'm sure you're aware that I came to Singapore to try and help Mrs. Motamboru."

Chang nodded. "Despite the evidence," he said, "I find it very difficult to think of that lady as guilty of murder."

"She isn't," Virgil said. "That's not wishful thinking on my part. If what I know now holds up, I should be able to prove it."

"I'm very happy to hear that, Mr. Tibbs. Your reputation is obviously well founded."

Tibbs ate a bite of the torte and found it the best he had ever tasted. "Mr. Chang," he said when he was ready, "I know without checking that a man in your position has to be capable of considerable discretion."

"I do have obligations," Chang admitted.

"And so do I, sir. With your cooperation, I'd like to confirm certain information that Mrs. Motamboru gave me."

"Suppose you tell me exactly what it is."

"First, she was an expected guest when she registered here."

"That's correct."

"She was given a suite on the twenty-second floor, which is, I understand, a diplomatic area."

Chang hesitated a bare moment. "That's also true, although we don't announce it publicly."

"Shortly after her arrival Mrs. Motamboru met with you privately. She stated that she was carrying a document of great importance and asked your help in seeing that it was especially protected."

"Obviously Madam Motamboru informed you fully about our conversation."

Virgil allowed himself one more bite of the succulent cake. "Yes, I believe she did. She also informed me that you took her document personally, gave her a receipt for it, and left your office. When you returned, you handed her a key. You told her at that time that if anyone but her presented the key, your security would be alerted immediately. Is this all correct so far?"

"Yes."

"You could testify to it in court?"

"If necessary."

"Later, when the key was used to open Mrs. Motamboru's box, it was found to be empty."

"That's correct."

"I have only one question, Mr. Chang. Let me put it confidentially. Does the vault have an inner section? One to which the public is never admitted?"

Chang paused before he answered. "Yes, it does. You would know why."

Tibbs set his plate back on the serving cart. "I suggest that this conversation remain between ourselves," he said, "and not be shared with anyone else without mutual agreement."

"I'm prepared to accept that," Chang said.

Virgil got to his feet. "Thank you for your time," he said.

The Straits Times reported that the police were conducting an intense investigation into the death of the Tan child. The paper was also correct when it added that the job was made much more difficult by the almost total absence of any clues.

Assistant Superintendent Lee was waiting anxiously for the lab reports on the material taken from the murder scene. The vacuuming had been done with meticulous care; if there had been anything at all to be found, the Scene of the Crime Unit would have gathered it up.

The reports, when they came in, were almost entirely

negative. None of the material submitted for examination had yielded anything significant. Lee accepted the verdict with a full sense of fatalism; he had almost literally prayed for a break, but the lab people had not been able to provide one.

Exhaustive interviews with other residents of the same block had produced nothing of value. One man, who had picked the wrong time to commit an offense, had been arrested on a charge of insulting the modesty of nineteen-year-old Miss Lui. The complainant reported that he had tried to put his arms around her without her permission. He admitted the charge and was booked.

When the phone rang in midafternoon in the Khe Bong Neighborhood Police Post, Inspector Cheng took the call personally. He identified himself and the location, then he waited, prepared for anything.

A harsh, almost rasping voice spoke in heavily accented Mandarin. "The Tan family had four children," the caller said. "Now they have two." Then he gave a short burst of almost demonic laughter before the line went dead.

Inspector Cheng had two very fast reactions. When the speaker had begun, he had been sure it was another crank call. He was fully prepared to deal with that, but when he heard the word *two* he instantly changed his mind. It could still be a crazy on the line, but the terrible possibility of that one word galvanized him into action.

He immediately sent a constable to check out the Tan apartment with all possible speed. Then he tried unsuccessfully to reach Lee, who was out in the field. Without hesitation he called Superintendent Subramaniam, the Homicide commander, and reported the conversation. The superintendent was equally alarmed by the context of the call. He ordered an immediate full check on the Tan family, with police protection if indicated. He also wanted to be informed of any more news the moment it came it.

With considerable presence of mind, Cheng put in a call to the Leong Shipyards and spoke to the chief of security. "You have an engineer, Tan Khin Peow," he began.

"The man whose daughter was murdered."

"Yes. This is nothing against him, but I need to know where he is right now and where he's been for the last hour. Anything at all you can give me about his movements today, I want."

"It is important, I assume."

"Most important."

"Is Engineer Tan under suspicion? Shall I take precautions?"

"No, but don't let him know about this conversation."

"I'll call you back." Cheng hung up; he had been speaking in Mandarin without realizing it.

The constable he had sent to the Tan apartment reported. "The door is locked and there is no one at home. At least I heard no sounds, and no one answered when I knocked."

He had barely finished speaking when Madam Wee Lai Chan, Tan's wife, came into the station. Like many of the residents of the Toa Payoh Housing Estate, she had taken a little while to become accustomed to the neighborhood police post, but now she was very grateful it was there.

As soon as she spoke her name, the desk man called Inspector Cheng and informed him of the visitor. Cheng came at once to see her. "Madam Wee," he said, and bowed slightly. With remarkably good sense he waited for the bereaved mother to tell him what was on her mind. When she did so, his blood almost froze.

"Inspector," she said. "Forgive me, sir, but my older son has not returned from school. He is very dutiful and almost never late. Because—of what has happened—I am very worried about him."

Chapter Ten

During the long night that followed, the Singapore Police searched intensively for the missing Tan boy. The investigation was headed by Lee, who ignored the fact that it was his small son's birthday to stay on the job for as long as was necessary.

He spread his net in all directions. Teams of officers searched all likely areas for the child. Despite the hour, he assigned detectives to seek out any possible enemies Tan or his wife might have. Every possibility, no matter how small or remote, was to be investigated. A second detective team began a further intensive questioning of the neighborhood people who had had any contact with the Tans. The shopkeepers with whom they usually dealt were located and questioned.

Woman Police Constable Ooi was detailed to stay with Madam Wee and her distraught husband, partly to lend moral support and also because she was multilingual. If a call were to come in to the Tan family in any likely language, she would be able to take it and report accurately on what had been said. For this purpose, she was authorized to impersonate Madam Wee on the telephone. A constable from the neighborhood police post was stationed in the hallway outside the apartment.

When he had done everything he possible could, Lee went himself to the Tan apartment. Madam Wee lay on her bed unable to control herself. W.P.C. Ooi was with her. Despite her relative inexperience, the female officer had the situation as much in hand as was possible under the circumstances. A neighbor, a close friend of the Tans, had come in to make tea and was busy in the tiny kitchen. Tan himself sat on the one much-used sofa, his hands clasped, his head bowed low. Lee quietly sat beside him.

"Mr. Tan," Lee said in his most understanding voice, "there are more than thirty men in search parties looking for your son. At the causeway to Malaysia, every car and truck is being searched. The harbor patrol has every available boat working. Traffic officers are combing the streets and checking vehicles."

Tan raised his head. "We are most grateful," he said.

Lee became confidential. "Mr. Tan, somewhere, for some reason, your family has a terrible enemy. Will you answer some questions for me?"

Tan nodded.

"This is not the time to hold back—to conceal anything; do you understand?"

Again Tan nodded.

"Mr. Tan, I will keep silent, but I must know if you belong to a secret society. You son's life may depend on your answer."

Tan shook his head. "I never joined any society," he said.

"Have you ever had any trouble with any society, or any of its members?"

"No, never."

"Only between ourselves, do you have a mistress? Don't be afraid to answer: I would have one myself, if I could afford it." That was a deliberate lie, but it was a means of establishing a rapport.

"No, not since I was married." He hesitated. "I have

two or three times had woman friends, very briefly, who were kind to me . . . but that was several years ago."

Lee nodded that he accepted the statement without censure.

"I must ask about your wife," Lee continued. "Have other men admired her?"

Again Tan shook his head. "She is a very good wife," he said. "She is not beautiful, but she is all that I ask. Other men do not bother her; she is too busy being a mother."

Lee hated what he had to do, but he kept on with his questioning.

"I ask that you trust me," he said, "and belive that I am trying my best to help you."

"I do," Tan said.

"If there is anything you have not told me, Mr. Tan, please tell me now. I give my word that anything you say will not be used against you."

Tan swallowed hard. "There is a woman at work," he said. "She wants me to leave my family and marry her. She is very persistent. I have told her *no* many times, but she refuses to accept that."

"I know how that can be," Lee said. "I have had the same problem. Only between ourselves, have you shared a bed with her?"

"No. If I did that, I would never get rid of her."

"Is she attractive?"

Tan straightened a little. "She has not the brains of a jellyfish."

Lee remembered that he was talking with a graduate engineer. "A woman scorned can be dangerous," he said. "I will have it looked into at once, without embarrassing you."

"I would be grateful, " Tan responded.

For another forty minutes Lee continued his questioning, but nothing more whatever came to light. He accepted a cup of tea from a fresh brewing. While he was drinking it, he looked in on Madam Wee. She appeared to be sleeping. "I gave her a sedative the doctor left last time," Miss Ooi said.

"A good idea," Lee agreed. He finished the tea, thanked the neighbor who had prepared it, and then went quickly back to the Khe Bong Police Post.

He was met at the door by Inspector Cheng, the watch commander. "Anything at all?" Lee asked.

Cheng shook his head. "Several couples having sex in secluded places," he answered. "I gave orders to ignore the incidents; we can't spare the time to process them."

"Agreed."

"Otherwise, nothing."

Lee went inside. "The boy cannot have evaporated," he said. "He will be found."

"What do you think are his chances?" Cheng asked. He was a young man who had come up through the ranks. Despite his lack of a degree, he was likely to go higher. He was an expert in hand-to-hand combat and taught at the Academy.

Lee did not equivocate. "I fear the worst," he said. "After the phone threat . . ." There was no need for him to finish.

The search for the missing Tan boy ended a few minutes after one in the morning. His body was discovered in a drainage ditch on the far northwest sector of the island. The Scene of the Crime Unit responded immediately, as did the necessary medical personnel. Lee made a decision not to tell the family until morning; he knew too much about the depressing effect of the small hours of the night.

He stayed on the job until the identification of the body was certain, then he stretched out on a cot in a small back room and was asleep almost at once.

*   *   *

An exceptionally grim meeting was held the following morning. There was a sharp tension in the air; every person present felt it. Deputy Commissioner Arthur Sim, a man of vast capability and experience, presided. He kept his manner relaxed and calm, but he was obviously deeply moved by the circumstances.

The group that surrounded him was made up of Assistant Superintendent Lee, Superintendent Subramaniam, who commanded the Homicide Division, Deputy Superintendent Dalip Singh, the head of the Scene of the Crime Unit, Inspector Cheng from the Khe Bong Police Post, and Superintendent Osman Bin Mohamed, the youthful-appearing, but very sharp head of the Prosecutions Division.

The meeting, as always, was conducted in English. At the deputy commissioner's direction, Lee summarized everything that was known up to that moment. He was precise and careful, and above all accurate. That did not preclude his offering his own opinions when he had finished his factual summary.

"I'm convinced that the father, Tan Khin Peow, is innocent," he said. "Most of the evidence so far tends to clear him, especially the phone call. I checked with the shipyard: Tan was in a meeting that lasted all afternoon. There is no way he could have made the call. Last night he was completely overcome with grief and worry. Olivier could not have acted the part as convincingly."

Deputy Commissioner Sim turned to Cheng. "What do you think?" he asked.

"I agree, sir. I know Tan well; he is a member of the residents' committee. He was very nearly in shock last night. Madam Wee, his wife, had to be sedated. I believe them both to be innocent victims."

The deputy commissioner did not know Cheng too well, but he did know Lee and respected his abilities. "We must assume, then, that an outside party or parties is responsible for these dreadful crimes," he said. "Pandian, what do you recommend?"

Subramaniam answered without hesitation. "I suggest a maximum effort on the background of the Tan family. There may be a rejected suitor for Madam Wee, before or after her marrage. Tan may have been promoted over someone's head. Even the children, innocent as they are, may have done something to bring intense hatred down on the whole family."

"Very sound," Sim said. "Has the Scene of the Crime Unit anything to give us yet?"

Dalip Singh was immaculate as always in his sharply pressed uniform and tightly wound green turban. "The lab work is not back yet," he said in his precise English, "but I do not expect great results. The preliminary medical report is that the boy was drowned in the ditch in which he was found. There were no indications of external injuries or sexual molestation. There were no surfaces to take prints, also no footprint evidence that we could find. We spent three hours at the scene, but we found nothing."

"What about the phone call?" Sim asked.

Inspector Cheng knew that was his cue. "First of all, sir, while it was fresh in my mind, I wrote down the exact words that were spoken."

"Excellent," Sim said.

"Here they are: *The Tan family had four children. Now they have two.* After that there was a demented kind of laugh before the line went dead. The caller spoke in Mandarin, but with a very strong accent."

"Just a moment," Sim interrupted. "Would you say that it was a genuine accent, or someone trying to fake one?"

"I can't answer that, sir," Cheng replied.

The deputy commissioner issued his instructions. "I want a constant watch kept over the Tan family," he said. "Get the necessary authority and have an extension of their phone with a recording device installed immediately in the Khe Bong Police Post. We're going to get a lot of calls on this, but I want every one of them followed up, no matter how improbable it may sound. If Madam Wee leaves her apartment, for any reason, she is to have a police escort. The same applies to the two remaining children. And I want every officer on duty, no matter what his assignment, to be alert for any kind of a break."

As the meeting broke up everyone present knew that this was one of the worst cases the Singapore Police had ever been called upon to face.

Virgil Tibbs was just about to go out when he received a call that he had a visitor. "Who is it?" he asked.

"Superintendent Lee, sir."

"Ask him to come right up."

A few moments later Lee tapped on the door, and Tibbs let him in. Lee looked around the elegant suite and shook his head a little sadly. "Tough having to live like this," he said.

"I manage," Tibbs answered. "How about some coffee?"

"I don't have the time," Lee answered, "I'm pushing things to come here as it is. Virgil, I want to have a serious talk with you."

Tibbs motioned for him to sit down and then took a chair close by.

"You know that my Western friends called me Roger," Lee began, "which makes things simpler. We weren't together very long in Pasadena, but during those few days I feel that we became friends."

"Absolutely," Tibbs agreed.

"Then I can talk plainly. Virgil, we're in a very tough spot right now and having you here could make it a lot worse."

"Do you want me to go home?" Virgil asked.

"No, not at all. But I think we have to make a deal. First

of all, you know that this Madam Motamboru business is a first-class headache for us. Why she had to come here I don't know, but she did, and we're stuck with her. Now on top of this we've got the Tan murders. Another of the children was killed last night, and the whole department is very uptight about it. I just came from a meeting at the deputy commissioner's office and it was pretty heavy."

"You say you wanted to make a deal," Tibbs prompted.

"Okay, Virgil, here it is. You talked to your friend, Mrs. Motamboru, and I presume she told you her whole story."

"I think so."

"You know, and I know, that it doesn't hold water. I'm not saying that the lady is lying, but she's been through some very tough times lately, and it's possible for her to be mistaken. Her claim that the man who came to her room isn't the same one who was found dead there is outside of reality. There were two maids at work just outside her suite at the time and they've been questioned exhaustively."

"You don't buy it, then," Tibbs said.

"No, we don't. Now, Virgil, we've got a very good and reliable witness, Dr. Singh. Have you talked to him yet?"

"No, but he's on my list."

"I can save you the trouble. He's a man of high reputation, an expert witness of the best kind. Dr. Singh is prepared to testify that he was called to attend Mrs. Motamboru right after the shooting. He examined her and discovered definite marks on her throat that she had been choked enough to render her unconscious. He will also testify that she had been given a drug, probably by injection."

"Can he name the drug?"

"No, there are several that would have done the trick. And he didn't want to take the liberty of examining her intimately enough to find the puncture mark. It was academic; she was already coming out of it."

"I think I see what you're driving at, Roger," Tibbs

said. "Miriam's story is too far out to be believed as it is. However, she could offer a strong case of self defense."

"Exactly!" Lee answered. "Now, Virgil, here's the deal. You know her well and I think she'll take your advice. No one knows her story except us, you're the only other person who's been allowed to see her, except the attorney who's been chosen to defend her. She can testify that a man was admitted to her suite and that he attacked her. Which is the absolute truth; I don't doubt that for a moment. He stabbed her with a needle; that's also true. So, in desperate self defense, she took her gun and shot him before she went out. On that basis the court can, and certainly will, find justifiable homicide, and she'll be off the hook. Your part is to persuade her to change her story."

Lee paused. "Dr. Singh's testimony will make her case, there's no doubt about it. I don't think she'll even be cross-examined, in view of who she is. In Singapore a woman's right to defend her honor is very strongly upheld."

Tibbs looked at his friend. "How much of this do you really believe?" he asked.

Lee gave him a straightforward look back. "Virgil, it's by far the most logical explanation. Remember, this woman was drugged; she may not remember firing the fatal shot at all. She may firmly believe she never did so. But in answer to your question, I can buy it. The lady goes free without any political backlash. You can go home, mission accomplished. What more do you want?"

Tibbs waited several moments, then he spoke. "Roger, the way you put it together it all makes sense. I don't know Singapore, but I can believe that the court will buy it. There's just one problem."

"Let's have it."

"If I were an attorney, I'd advise her to cop that plea. But I don't think it's the truth."

"You mean, you believe her story as she tells it now?"

"Yes. There's more to this, and I want to investigate further."

Lee got to his feet. "All right, that's your option, at least until her case comes up. But let me give you some advice: if you want to see any of our people, particulary those in command positions, call me first and let me pave the way. This Tan thing has got everyone on edge."

He stopped for a moment more. "Virgil, I've got to tell you that some people in the department frankly resent your being here. They'll never let you know it, but having an outsider come in to show them how to do their jobs is causing a lot of talk. That's why I want you to clear any appointments with me first."

"I will," Tibbs promised.

Lee dropped a folder on the sofa. "There's a copy of our file on the Motamboru case," he said. "I got permission to show it to you. But keep your mouth shut about it and from now on, Virgil, watch your step whatever you do."

Chapter Eleven

For the rest of that day Virgil Tibbs was a very busy man. First of all he got in touch with Janice Oliver at the American embassy and asked a favor of her. When he also supplied the reason for his request, she was quite willing to cooperate. Next he called at the offices of four airlines and in each case persuaded the local manager to assist him with some specific information. The airline people, after he had taken them partway into his confidence, were most helpful.

He then called the women's prison, spoke with someone in authority, and requested that Miriam Motamboru be asked a single question. He waited almost ten minutes until a matron came back on the line with the answer. Armed with the additional information he had received, he began to place a series of long-distance calls. In Switzerland there was a distinct reluctance to answer any of his questions until he suggested that the American embassy be consulted as to his status. His membership in the International Police Association proved to be of considerable value, and he did not hesitate to make use of it.

That evening, after a somewhat sparse dinner, he sat down with the official file on the Motamboru case and went through it in meticulous detail, over and over, until he virtually knew it by heart. He went to bed late, slept not very well, and woke up early, anxious to get to the main public library as soon as it was open. Because he now had a number of irons in the fire, he left word with the hotel operator where he could be located if necessary.

He was called to the phone shortly after eleven. When he responded, he was informed by a cultured female voice that Deputy Commissioner Sim would be pleased if Mr. Tibbs could join him for lunch. Since that invitation had to be accepted, Virgil did so and was informed that a car would pick him up at his hotel at twelve-thirty.

From a public phone booth he called Roger Lee and asked for a briefing. Lee told him to proceed to the Crossroads, and he would call him there. Hardly twenty minutes later Tibbs was back in his suite, preparing himself for what he knew would be a very important appointment. He was relieved when the phone rang.

"You know why I didn't want to talk to you from my office," Lee said. "You'll find Arthur Sim a very congenial gentleman, but he can be tough as nails when he has to. He's also very smart; don't be fooled because he won't let it show. He's one of the top cops in Asia. The commissioner has so many political and diplomatic duties, Sim does most of the day-to-day running of the department."

"So I'm going to have to keep my face on straight," Tibbs said.

"Damn right," Lee agreed, and hung up.

At twelve-thirty on the dot an unmarked police car pulled into the driveway of the Crossroads. Tibbs was ready, dressed in the best suit he owned. He was driven to one of the new high rises that fill the Singapore skyline and directed to the top floor. A swift and silent elevator took him up. When the door slid open he was at the entrance to an obviously elegant restaurant.

He was met there by Arthur Sim, who introduced himself without pretension. The deputy commissioner was slightly under six feet and perfectly groomed in an obviously expensive hand-tailored suit. He appeared to be somewhere in his fifties, but despite his cordial manner, there was an air of authority about him that could not be mistaken. "Thank you so much for coming," he said. "I know it was very short notice."

"I'm honored," Tibbs replied.

A slim hostess, made more so by the Chinese gown she wore, showed them to a window table facing south. Tibbs paused before sitting down to drink in the breathtaking view.

There before him was a vast, 180-degree panorama of the island city: its buildings, its streets, its shipyards, and its compelling harbor. Fifty to a hundred vessels were anchored within easy sight, while a swarm of smaller vessels and lighters wove their separate paths to and around them. Farther out several islands were visible, accented by scattered cumulus clouds that seemed to hang suspended just above the water. From hundreds of feet below, the subdued sounds of the city could just be heard.

The deputy commissioner waited while his guest absorbed the spectacular view. At last Tibbs sat down and unfolded the immaculate napkin that lay at his place. "Pardon me," he said, "but I've never seen anything to equal that. Not anywhere."

Sim seemed pleased with the comment. "It's an endlessly changing picture, Mr. Tibbs. On a good day you can see almost to Indonesia. It's like looking at a living map."

A waiter in a freshly pressed maroon suit handed Tibbs a large bound menu. The prices were in Singapore dollars, but when Virgil mentally changed them into American money, they were still almost as spectacular as the view. "Would you care for bird's nest soup?" Sim asked.

"Would I offend you if I made another choice?" Tibbs

asked. "I don't believe I'm in a position yet to appreciate that delicacy."

Sim smiled. "Choose whatever you like; everything here is quite good. I believe this restaurant might approach the American standard."

This time Virgil smiled, a little grimly. "There are very few cities in America that could boast of anything like this," he said. "It must be a gourmet's heaven."

"It does enjoy a good reputation locally. Please, Mr. Tibbs, don't try to be polite: order what you would really like. I can recommend a luncheon steak; the best Australian beef is flown in."

"Then I'll have one," Tibbs said.

When the order had been placed, Sim leaned back with a deceptively relaxed manner. When he spoke his voice was casual. "I do hope you're enjoying your visit here."

"Very much," Tibbs answered. "I went to Kathmandu once; otherwise my traveling has been very limited. So this is a new experience."

For several minutes the conversation remained casual. Since the deputy commissioner was the host, Tibbs was careful to follow his lead and for the time being stayed away from anything official.

"You know that you're looking at the second-busiest port in the world," Sim said, "one that has some interesting police problems at times. We just concluded one recently."

Tibbs took his cue. "Please tell me about it," he invited.

"We had a series of ship sinkings, with heavy losses in each case. They all took place on the open sea, where the only witnesses were the survivors. The instances were scattered over a period of time, but we suspected that the ships were being deliberately scuttled."

"For the insurance claims?"

"Yes. What put us onto it was the lack of any loss of life. When a ship goes down at sea, it is not too often that the whole crew survives unhurt, but in these instances not a single person was lost or even seriously injured."

Tibbs thought for a moment. "Is it possible that the ships could have been loaded with substitute cargo, or less than was on their manifests?"

"We suspected that, but no matter how diligently we questioned the ships' officers and crew members in each case, we were never able to find out anything. We also came up dry when we tried to investigate on the docks. Everyone declared that the ships had been loaded exactly according to their manifests. If fraud was involved, then obviously every crew member, as well as many shore-based people, had to be in on it.

"How did you crack it?" Tibbs asked.

The deputy commissioner offered a smile with a certain amount of guile in it. "By means of bird's nest soup."

Tibbs waited a moment. "I presume you mean that literally," he said.

"Yes," Sim answered, "quite literally. As we were just discussing, bird's nest soup is a widely known Chinese delicacy. There is quite an industry gathering real bird's nests for the purpose. According to her manifest, the last ship to go down was carrying five tons of bird's nests. That quantity represented a very high value."

"I would suggest, sir, that it also represented an impossibility," Tibbs said.

"Why?"

"I don't know the weight of an average bird's nest, but it couldn't be more than two or three ounces."

"That's it exactly. We computed the number of nests it would take to make up five tons. To secure such a quantity would be virtually impossible, even for the people whose ancestors built the Great Wall. When we pre-

98

sented our findings to the shipping people, the air became harmonious."

"You mean they sang."

"Indeed they did. Ah, here comes our luncheon."

Conversation ceased while the food was flawlessly served. Although Tibbs had not ordered iced tea, a tall glass with just enough ice was placed before him. The steak was generous in size and perfectly cooked medium rare, as he liked it. For a short while he devoted himself exclusively to eating; the last meal of such quality he had been given had been prepared for him by Miriam Motamboru.

When he deemed that the time was ripe, he took the initiative. "I'd like to ask a question, if I may," he said.

"Certainly."

"How high do I have to go to get Mrs. Motamboru out of jail?"

Sim was unruffled. "We don't enjoy having her on our hands, but to release her we would need some firm evidence in support of her innocence. Also someone willing to guarantee her appearance in court when the time comes."

"Would you consider me suitable for that?"

"How would you protect her?"

"I'd put her back in her suite at the Crossroads and look after her personally. I've had some experience in that role."

"Yes, we know about that, of course. There are separate bedrooms in the suite, so I presume the management would approve. You realize that appearances mean a great deal in this case. But first there's the matter of evidence."

Tibbs took his time with his steak and the best french fries he had ever eaten. When he was ready, he picked his moment carefully and spoke without emphasis. "I can prove she's innocent," he said.

Chapter Twelve

Sim looked about the room and then got up. "Please excuse me a moment," he said. "I see someone I know."

Tibbs sat quietly in his chair, looking out the window beside him at the exotic tropical panorama that was, to him, the other side of the world. The far distance that he could see, perhaps to the equator and beyond, sent a hard-to-define sensation running up his spine. Millions dreamt of far distant travel; at that moment it had come true for him. He was thousands of miles from home, as far south as Brazil, in a place where the people were different, the religions were different, and oriental languages predominated. His host's English was flawless, but Chinese was undoubtedly his mother tongue.

He could not help realizing how far out of his own element he was—in terms of culture, local knowledge, and also law enforcement. Even such a simple reference as 459 for burglary would not be understood here. The people who talked to him all had to speak what was to them a foreign language. No matter how fluent they were, there was an inescapable difference.

He turned his attention back to the room when he saw Sim returning with another man. Automatically he stood up for the introduction to be performed. "Mr. Tibbs," the deputy commissioner said with a touch of formality. "I'd like you to meet a very dear friend of mine, Judge Goh Poh-kee. Poh-kee, this is Virgil Tibbs."

"How do you do, Your Honor," Tibbs acknowledged.

"I've taken the liberty of inviting Judge Goh to join us," Sim added. "I hope you don't mind."

"Certainly not; I'm delighted," Tibbs replied. In a matter of seconds the maître d' was supervising the laying of an additional place at the table.

The judge was a distinguished-appearing man with a full head of black hair tinged with white at the sides. His features were essentially Chinese, but they appeared to have a certain universal cast that transcended the boundaries of any one segment of humanity. Tibbs guessed that he was about sixty, but his face was unlined and there were no pouches under his eyes. "I'm delighted to meet you, Mr. Tibbs," the judge said. "Of course I'd heard of your arrival."

The judge's luncheon plate was quickly placed on the table, new silverware was provided, and a fresh glass of ice water was set at the right. A waiter held his chair while he sat down. The whole operation was done with notable smoothness and ease, another indication to Tibbs that he was in an absolutely top-rank establishment.

Sim looked toward his friend. "Just before you joined us, Mr. Tibbs made a most interesting statement. He said that he can prove that Madam Motamboru is innocent of the charges laid against her."

The judge accepted that without expression. "As it happens, Mr. Tibbs," he said, "following her arrest Madam Motamboru appeared before me. I examined the available evidence at the time and ordered her held for trial without bail. That was strictly according to our code of justice. In view of her position, I very much regretted having to do that, but you will appreciate that there were many considerations involved."

"Including the good name of Singapore," Tibbs said.

The judge inclined his head.

"May I ask a question, Your Honor?"

"Of course."

"If I am able to satisfy you of her innocence while we are here, and that at the appropriate time I will provide the necessary hard evidence, would that be enough to have her freed?"

"Assuming that you are able to do that, Mr. Tibbs, I would be happy to sign the release order immediately. However, there would have to be certain restrictions."

"Fully understood, sir. I'll give my personal guarantee that she won't leave the country or in any way impede the judicial process."

"Then I'm most interested," the judge said.

"Thank you, Your Honor. And thank you for taking the trouble to come and meet with us here today." Tibbs turned toward the deputy commissioner. "Forgive me, sir, but I have a policeman's suspicion of too-convenient coincidences."

When Sim showed no reaction at all, the judge filled the gap. "I'm sure, Mr. Tibbs, that we are most anxious to hear what you have to say." He cut a piece of his fillet of sole.

Tibbs began very calmly. "Gentlemen, I want you to know that I appreciate your position. An unexpected case lands in your lap, one involving a foreign lady of high position who's accused of murder. It's a delicate matter, to be dealt with carefully and diplomatically. Then you learn that a policeman from another jurisdiction, several thousand miles away, is coming here to get into the act, as we say at home."

"I see your point," the deputy commissioner said, "but we are still very happy to welcome you."

"Sir," Tibbs replied, "I don't believe that if you received word that Sherlock Holmes himself had found someone to look after his bees, and was en route to Sin-

102

gapore to assist here, you would be overjoyed."

Sim relaxed enough to smile. "I have to dispute you there, Mr. Tibbs," he said. "I would be delighted to meet Sherlock Holmes under any circumstances."

"I'm sorry, sir," Tibbs continued, "that I'm not in that league. My only advantage is that I know Mrs. Motamboru quite well. I interviewed her here at some length. In doing so I learned that despite her intelligence, she was expertly conned from the moment she arrived in Switzerland. It was made easier because she must have been in a very distressed state of mind. I'm sure you're familiar with her story."

"I think we are," the judge said.

"Then you know she was carrying a very important document that her husband had promised to the President."

Sim merely nodded.

"Mrs. Motamboru told me that when she arrived in Geneva she was met at the airport by a man purportedly from the American embassy. He promptly put her on a flight to Zurich, where he had made a reservation for her at a first-class hotel. He advised her that she would be safer there. As soon as she had told me that much, I definitely knew that something was wrong."

He stopped and took a drink of water. "If the embassy had sent someone to meet her on arrival, then whoever was in charge would certainly have wanted to see her. It made no sense at all to hustle her off to Zurich at the other end of the country. And the statement that she would be safer there is ridiculous. Geneva is a city of international importance that has to be well policed."

Virgil stopped to eat another mouthful of his rapidly cooling steak.

"Yesterday I asked our embassy here to check with Geneva. Miss Janice Oliver will confirm that Geneva did not know Mrs. Motamboru was arriving and obviously didn't

103

send anyone to meet her. I then confirmed that she was on the next flight to Zurich; her name is on the manifest, and two of the stewardesses specifically remember her. Flight operations was kind enough to check for me."

"Why do you think she was sent to Zurich?" Sim asked.

"To keep her away from the American embassy, or any of its staff. Next I checked with the hotel in Zurich. The reservation was made by an anonymous caller, not by the American embassy."

"How did you know which hotel?" the judge asked.

"I called the jail and they asked Mrs. Motamboru. Now, according to her story, the man who met her in Geneva called on her early the following morning. That didn't make sense either. The United States has representatives available in Zurich, but the same man showed up, almost indecently early. When I checked the airline schedules yesterday, I learned there was a later flight he could have taken from Geneva to Zurich, and that there were seats available.

"Mrs. Motamboru told me that they had breakfast together in her room. It was not her idea: her visitor ordered it sent up before he presented himself. I verified that. He told her she was to proceed to Singapore where 'special arrangements would be made.' He explained that the Swiss are very particular about their neutrality. On the face of it that was preposterous. If the purpose had been to get her to an American ambassador as soon as possible, there were several embassies in Europe very much nearer than Singapore."

"You will excuse me," the judge said, "but I have to consider the possibility that Madam Motamboru made much of this up."

"Of course, Your Honor," Tibbs replied, "but please note that I've personally verified everything I've told you so far, and I can produce witnesses. The concierge on duty at the time definitely remembers that a gentleman came to see her early that morning. Of course he could have been protecting her reputation, but he specifically mentioned that the visitor placed the breakfast order, which was unusual. He was very clear on that point when I talked to him."

Tibbs took time to eat another mouthful and drank some iced tea.

"Unless she had been advised to do so, there is no rational reason why she would have come here to Singapore. May I also point out that telling her she should leave because the Swiss are very touchy about their neutrality was absurd: there was no issue of neutrality concerned, though she was led to believe so at the time."

Virgil cut one more bite of steak and ate it, even though it was by then nearly cold. "There is another point, gentlemen, that came out when I interviewed her. Mrs. Motamboru said that although the people at the hotel in Zurich knew who she was, she registered under an assumed name. The hotel was reluctant to discuss it at first, but an assistant manager, Mr. Lindholm, has now confirmed that as correct."

"It was a reasonable thing for her to do," the judge contributed. "To avoid unwanted press attention, or other publicity."

"Thank you, sir," Tibbs said. "I'm bringing this up because later in our interview, I asked Mrs. Motamboru if it wouldn't have been simpler, since the document was in a totally safe place, to wait until the ambassador returned. She told me that had been her plan, but her visitor had convinced her that time was of the essence. Let me quote her exactly. 'I had already received a message from Bakara asking me to come home.' That was a dead giveaway: there is no way anyone in Bakara could have known where she was, or the name under which she was registered."

Sim's attitude had visibly mellowed a little. "I begin to

understand your reputation, Mr. Tibbs," he said.

Virgil did his best to let that pass. "It was only after that, she consented to come to Singapore. She was given a first-class ticket and told that an American agent would contact her on the plane out of Bangkok. Through our embassy here I learned that no American agent to their knowledge had been scheduled to meet with Mrs. Motamboru."

"She could have invented that episode," the judge said.

"True, sir," Tibbs countered, "but there was no reason for her to do so. The indisputable fact is that she did arrive here in Singapore, which greatly supports her story. Also, she checked into the hotel where a reservation had been made for her."

"By whom?" Sim asked.

"The hotel records don't show, sir. Only that it was made directly and no travel agent's commission was involved."

The judge ate the last bite of his fish and took his time chewing it before he spoke. "Mr. Tibbs, you have certainly created a reasonable doubt. However, I'm still faced with the fact that Madam Motamboru was found behind the locked door of her suite with the body of a man who had been shot with her gun. A man she claims she had never met."

Sim spelled it out. "That, you understand, Mr. Tibbs, is the crux of the matter. If you can explain that, I would be very much interested."

Tibbs wiped his lips with his napkin. "She also told me the body found in her suite was not that of the man who had originally called on her. I know that sounds impossible, and I fully understand why you couldn't believe her. But if it could be established as true, then, if you will pardon the Americanism, it's a whole new ball game."

The judge leaned forward a little, the expression on his face subtly changed. "I want to ask you something, Mr. Tibbs," he said. "Are you convinced that Mrs. Motamboru is a truthful person?"

"Without reservation," Tibbs answered.

"Do you have any idea at all how such an exchange might have been accomplished?"

"I have much more work to do before I'll be prepared to answer that, Your Honor," Tibbs replied. "But I do know which direction I'm going to go."

Chapter Thirteen

From his luncheon meeting Tibbs went directly to the morgue. He was upset with himself; in front of two very important men he had probably expounded too much. No one likes a smart aleck: he hoped to high heaven they hadn't seen him in that light. Obviously they had doubted Miriam's story, as any sane person who didn't know her would. He did know her; that had given him a temporary advantage. His fear was that he might have exploited it too much.

At the morgue he talked with an Indian gentleman who listened gravely to what he had to say and then called the Central Police Building. He spent some time on the phone before he hung up. "I am instructed to extend you every courtesy within reasonable limits," he said. "This includes the post mortem photographs of the body found in the Crossroads Hotel. Are you accustomed to viewing such material?"

"Very accustomed," Tibbs answered. "I'm the principal homicide investigator for the Pasadena Police Department."

The Indian gave him a sad-eyed look. "It would have aided matters if you had told me that in the beginning," he said. "Please wait." He left, to return presently with a large official envelope in his hands. He handed it over and then sat patiently while Tibbs went through the contents.

It took him several minutes to study each photograph in detail; meanwhile the Indian sat very still and observed. When he had finished, Virgil separated the grim prints into two piles, one of which he handed back. "Thank you for showing these to me," he said. "They were very informative. There were several things about this case I had not been told."

The Indian accepted the prints. "And the other photographs?" he asked.

"If possible, I would like to borrow them for a short while."

"They are not to be given or shown to the press."

"Of course not," Tibbs agreed.

The Indian put them in an envelope. "If you would be kind enough to sign a receipt . . ."

From the morgue Tibbs took a taxi to the American embassy. Janice Oliver was out, but the credential he carried promptly got him in to see a sandy-haired young man whose dress and demeanor suggested one of the Ivy League colleges. After Tibbs had stated his business, the young man picked up a phone. "I have Mr. Virgil Tibbs here. He has asked for access to some confidential material." After that simple statement he listened momentarily and then put the phone down. "Mr. Myers will see you shortly," he said.

Tibbs sat quietly and refrained from small talk for a good ten minutes while the young man, not too urgently, gave attention to the papers on his desk. Then the door opened and an older man, whose casual appearance did not suggest a diplomat, came into the office. Without speaking he beckoned with his hand for Tibbs to follow him. Obediently Virgil got up and left without looking back. The young man kept on with his work.

The older, heavier-set man, who was definitely balding, led the way to a small office that was strictly functional; no effort at all had been spent on decor. The man did not introduce himself or offer to shake hands. "What do you have?" he asked.

Tibbs handed over the basic I.D. he had been given. His host looked at it and then handed it back. "That doesn't do it," he said.

Tibbs reached for his wallet again and took out his emergency credential. He knew that this was not an emergency in the strict sense of the term, but he could not afford to be stymied at that point.

The second credential made more of an impression. The man looked at it carefully, then with it in his hand, he left the room without explanation. He crossed the hall to a door that he had to use a combination lock to open. Inside there were three CRT monitors, several keyboards, and other equipment. He put the card he was carrying into a small cubical machine that swallowed it and then projected a number on a screen together with a photograph that had not been visible on its surface.

The man studied the photograph for a moment or two, then he sat down at one of the keyboards and put in the number shown on the screen. Within a few seconds a panel of data was displayed. The man read each item carefully before he shut down the equipment and went back to where Tibbs was waiting.

He handed back the card and then sat behind his desk in a much more relaxed manner. "Jason Myers, Virgil," he said.

"Do you know why I'm here?"

"Yes. I've been expecting you. Any hope you can get her out of it?"

"It's possible. I just had lunch with Arthur Sim."

Myers shifted in his chair. "Watch yourself there. He has a very agreeable manner, but he's extremely sharp. Nothing gets by him: nothing at all."

"I gathered that. He let me tell him some things I'm sure he already knew. He took me to a lavish restaurant to size me up. I think he's a good cop."

"Hell yes, Virgil; no doubt about that. Now how can I help you?"

Tibbs handed over the morgue photographs. Myers glanced through them and passed them back. "Have the police I.D.'d him yet?"

Tibbs caught the tone of his voice. "Was he one of ours?"

"Yes. A good friend of mine."

"I'd like whatever you can give me on him with what I'm carrying."

"There's one thing I don't know, and that's how he got himself into that damned hotel suite. Not because of the locked door, that's no problem at all, but without being seen. There were two maids working right outside."

"One vacuuming, the other making up a room," Tibbs supplied.

"That's right. And it's certain they've been thoroughly checked out. There's a very bright guy named Lee in charge of the case. Sim has his eye on him."

"Lee is a friend of mine; I met him in the States."

"That's a leg up for you. He's a good man, and he won't stab you. Coffee?"

"No thanks. What can you give me on the dead man?"

"It has to be strictly QT."

"I know."

"His name was Jim Ramsey. He'd been in Africa for the past year or more; he was our private pipeline to Motamboru. Damned good at it too. Madam didn't recognize him when she saw the body."

"Are we investigating?"

"Yes. We've got a hot agent on it right now. You."

Tibbs kept silent for a moment. "Am I working for the Company?" he asked.

111

"If you were, you'd know it. No, we're piggy-backing for the moment. Anything else I can help with?"

"Explain something. I noticed that every time I referred to the lady as Mrs., they always came back with Madam. Is that because of her position?"

Myers folded his hands behind his head. "No, Virgil. Here every married woman is called madam, no matter who she is. Something else that might confuse you: Married women generally keep their own names. If Miss Wong marries Mr. Ho, she isn't called Mrs. Ho; she becomes Madam Wong. Westerners seldom get that right."

Virgil stood up. "Thanks, Jason."

"Jack."

"I'll probably have to come back."

"Anytime."

From the embassy Virgil went directly to the main Singapore library. There for some time he devoted himself to studying the recent history of Bakara. He made pages of notes on a long yellow legal pad he had brought with him. When he at last looked at his watch, it was past six.

Regretfully he turned in the material he was using and headed back to the Crossroads. He was not very hungry after the substantial lunch he had had, but it was time to eat something. The Singapore Symphony Orchestra was giving a concert that evening and, assuming he could get a ticket, he planned to go.

He picked up his key at the desk and rode up to the suite that was much too large for his requirements. He was not used to such luxurious surroundings, but he was willing to enjoy them while he could.

As soon as he opened the door he saw Miriam Motamboru, standing in the center of the room, waiting for him. She had on a simple but beautifully designed batik dress. Once more she was the poised and remarkable woman he had known while he had posed as her husband.

112

His first impulse was to seize her in his arms, but the restraints he had once built up held him back.

Miriam sensed his feelings. "Thank you for getting me out of jail," she said.

"I'm very glad to see you," he responded. It was totally inadequate, but his usual poise had momentarily deserted him.

"Just before four this afternoon they told me I was to be released—in your custody."

Virgil got hold of himself. "That's very good news," he said.

She came to him and put her hands on his shoulders. "Here I am," she offered.

The months that had passed since he had guarded her in Pasadena vanished as he gathered her in. He remembered not to crush her too hard against him, but the warm softness of her body was a strong temptation. He knew she desperately needed someone to cling to: someone to relieve her of the fearful burden she had been carrying.

He held her a long time before he released her and let her sit down. "Since there's two bedrooms, do you mind if we share this suite?"

"No," Miriam answered. "Of course not."

"Then I'll move my stuff."

"You don't have to; the hotel people took care of it. Mr. Chang had my things brought up; that's why I was able to dress decently for you. He's invited us for dinner; will you accept?"

Tibbs had fully recovered his poise. "Of course. At what time?"

"Seven-thirty."

"Then I'll go and freshen up."

"Virgil, I want to talk to you first."

He turned and sat down, giving her his full attention.

"When I was first arrested, the American ambassador

113

came to see me. He offered to do anything for me he could. So I asked for you. I didn't realize how selfish that was. I've made you leave your work and come halfway around the world, just to help me. Please forgive me."

He tried to speak, but she silenced him with a hand. "Virgil, I was raised very well. The question never came up, but my family is quite wealthy. That's how they were able to send me to the Sorbonne and to so many other places. I was kept away from people who would avoid me . . . because of my heritage. I was never exposed to prejudice. I'm afraid that you were."

"As a boy, yes, and some when I was in school," Tibbs admitted. "Never in the police department."

"Another thing: I remember how careful you were, how self-disciplined, when we were living in the same house. That's something no woman would ever forget. That's why I trust you so much."

"I came here because I wanted to," Tibbs said. "I'm glad I was given the chance." That was the literal truth. "I just want us to stay friends." He didn't allow himself to go beyond that.

Miriam looked at him with the calm poise of a woman who knows her own mind. "For as long as you like," she said.

That was almost too much for Tibbs, after what he had already been through that day. He wanted to respond, but the right words would not come.

A small stab of pain in his side brought him back to reality. "If you'll excuse me," he said, "I'd better get ready for dinner."

"Of course," Miriam answered. She watched him carefully as he retreated to the bedroom that was now his.

The evening was still relatively young when the call came in to the Khe Bong Police Post. The sergeant who took it gave a quick glance at the voice-actuated recorder to be sure that it was on before he answered briskly in Chinese and then briefly in English.

Although he had not heard it before, he knew it was the same voice. Once more it rasped in uncertain Mandarin. "The Tan family has two children. One from two is one." A low, harsh laugh followed. The unearthly sound ended when the connection was broken.

The sergeant immediately dispatched two constables to the Tan apartment on the double. Using every available man, he threw a cordon around the ground exits from the building with firm instructions that no one was be allowed either in or out. No one at all on any pretext whatever. That took only a few seconds. Then he called Central Police Headquarters and reported.

Reinforcements arrived rapidly and in strength. The first break was the news that the Tan family was at home and that both of their children were there and safe. Two husky constables were stationed outside their door. No one not known to them to be a police officer was to be admitted; even the kindly neighbor who had brewed tea the last time was excluded.

Assistant Superintendent Lee was reached by beeper at the symphony concert. He hurried out, to the consternation of others who had to get up to let him past in the midst of an exquisite andante by Mozart. When he reached a telephone, he was vastly relieved to learn that both of the surviving Tan children were safe at home and that full police protection had been swiftly laid on. He responded to the scene in his own car and spent the next four hours of the night in decisive but frustrated action.

Inspector Cheng, who had taken the first call, listened carefully to the tape and confirmed that it was the same voice. "I'll never forget it—never," he declared. Experienced policeman that he was, he could not keep his voice from shaking.

The Tan family was hurriedly taken in an unmarked police car to an unstated destination. W.P.C. Ooi was located and brought in; she had established a good rapport with Madam Wee, Tan's wife, and was well liked by the children. The family was installed in a small home that was actually police property and equipped with certain sophisticated security devices. By then Madam Wee was unable to control herself, and her husband was not very much better.

Constable Ooi, who was called Irene by her Caucasian friends, showed remarkable cool-headedness and efficiency. She saw the children tucked into unfamiliar beds with an encouraging smile. She served tea and sweetcakes as though she were a hostess in her own home. As she did so, she emphasized that this time the police had things totally under control and that the children were safe. She explained that the house was wired and that no one could possibly gain entry without setting off a battery of alarms. Even though the location was secret, full coverage would be given throughout the night by plainclothes officers. In some part reassured, Tan and his wife went to bed.

It was not until three in the morning that their surviving daughter began to show the first signs of having been poisoned.

Chapter Fourteen

When Ooi Lay Kim had announced her intention of join-
ing the police force, her family had been stunned by the
remote possibility that she might be accepted. During all
of her long and arduous training at the Academy, they patiently waited for the day when she would have had enough
and would resign. Less desirable would be to have her
dropped from the cadet ranks for lack of performance, for
that would have involved loss of face, but no well-bred and
-brought up Chinese girl with a university education had
any business out doing strenuous exercises in the blazing
hot sun and rappeling down the sides of multistoried
buildings. She would never find a desirable husband that
way.

They did reluctantly attend a swimming meet held in
the Academy's magnificent Olympic-size pool. There they
discovered that their daughter had also become a shark in
the water, good enough to be mentioned as a possibility
for Singapore in the Asian Games.

At the appointed time Lay Kim, whom many barbarian
people indecently called Irene, graduated with honors and
became a Woman Police Constable. Against his nature and
all of his traditions, her father managed to be slightly proud
of her. Totally out of his ken was the fact that she had ac-
quired a non-Chinese boyfriend. Their relationship ap-

peared to be entirely platonic, but he found it difficult to bear this humiliation silently. And when she outraged all decency by permitting herself to be kissed, and in a public place, he felt strongly that the end of the world, as he knew it, was near. He should never have permitted her to be educated.

Although Lay Kim had not chosen to follow the old traditions, she had a strong sense of duty and real dedication to her career in the police. While the Tan family lay sleeping in their temporary quarters, she remained awake and alert. She had been assigned to look after the children inside the house: to her that meant a continuous watch. Therefore the moment that the surviving little Tan girl began to show the first symptoms of distress, Lay Kim was at her side within seconds. When she saw the child's strained features and heard her labored breathing, she picked up her little police radio and reported it at once.

The sergeant in charge of the protection detail was equally efficient: he made an immediate call for an ambulance and a doctor. Irene Ooi was still new on the force, but she had already earned his respect. He knew he might be overreacting, but in this situation he did not dare to take the slightest chance.

When the medical help arrived minutes later, Constable Ooi had the parents up and was herself doing an efficient job of administering first aid. The doctor made a quick careful examination of his little patient, gave her an injection, and ordered her to be taken immediately to the hospital. With lights flashing the ambulance pulled away under police escort.

Following the doctor's orders, Constable Ooi administered a sedative to the almost frantic parents. The drug had not had time to take effect when Assistant Superintendent Lee arrived on the scene. The sergeant in charge reported that Lay Kim's diligence and prompt action could very well have saved the little Tan girl's life. Lee thanked

Lord Buddha for that and then faced the difficult task of questioning the parents once again.

Lee did his utmost to be considerate, but he had to get the information he desperately needed. What had the little girl eaten? What had she been given? Where had she been that someone had been able to give her poison?

He did not have much time before the sedative took effect and he had to stop. At that moment Constable Ooi put a hot, relaxing cup of tea in his hand and won his undying gratitude. He suddenly realized that she was very attractive. She was slightly moon-faced, as many Chinese girls are, but her exceptional character made her as lovely as the Japanese, Kojima Akiko, who had become Miss Universe.

When the land line telephone rang, he picked it up immediately. "Lee," he said, and waited for whatever fateful news he was to hear. Central Police Headquarters reported that the Tan child had had her stomach pumped, never a pleasant ordeal, but she was considered out of danger. Another half-hour would have been too late.

With a sense of great relief in his heart, Lee conveyed the good news to Tan and his wife. He added that Constable Ooi had certainly saved their child's life. He would see that she received an official commendation for her diligence and prompt, effective actions.

Madam Wee embraced Lay Kim, silently expressing her gratitude. Then Tan hugged her and so far forgot himself that he planted a grateful kiss on her cheek. Lay Kim gave it right back as tears rolled down her cheeks.

Lee turned toward Tan and his wife. "One thing I promise you," he said in Mandarin, "I'll get that offspring of a diseased tiger if it's the last act of my life.

Virgil Tibbs awoke shortly after seven in the morning. He had at last overcome the jet lag that had been pestering him since his arrival. He shaved, showered, and dressed with an acute awareness that Miriam Motamboru was in the other end of the suite and he would most likely be spending a good part of the day with her.

When he was ready, he went into the living room. Miriam was quietly sitting there, dressed in a white pantsuit that emphasized the smooth and very feminine lines of her figure. She got to her feet with a smile. "Good morning," she said. "Did you sleep well?"

"Surprisingly well," Tibbs answered. "Knowing you were out of jail was a big help."

"Shall I have breakfast sent up?"

"Why don't we go down and eat," Virgil suggested.

"I should know that I can't spoil you," Miriam said. "Before we go, I think you'd better tell me what I'm allowed to do and what not. And about any reports I have to make."

"Technically, you're still under suspicion of murder," he answered. "It was a major concession that they let you out. I guaranteed that you wouldn't leave the country or do anything to interfere with their judicial process."

"What you're saying, Virgil, is that I'm still in jail in theory if not in fact."

"That's right, Miriam."

"Can I go shopping?"

"Of course. Take sightseeing tours—anything like that. But I'd suggest that you stay away from the causeway up to Malaysia, the airport, and the dock area."

"I see. Don't allow any suspicion that I'm trying to leave."

"Exactly. Remember, Miriam, that although this is a very racially mixed community, we will still stand out."

"Virgil, would it bother you if I stayed rather close to you for a day or two? I'm accustomed to getting along on my own almost anywhere, but right now I'm a little shaken."

"Of course you are. I want you to stay close, because I'm going to need you with me today."

120

"What are we going to do?"

"Help to prove that you're not guilty of murder," Tibbs said. "Let's go down and have breakfast."

They ate in the coffee shop with tourists filling most of the spaces around them. There was a more elegant dining room open, but it was not the right time to patronize it—something that Miriam understood completely. When they had finished and Tibbs had signed the check, he went to a telephone and phoned the Central Police Building.

Assistant Superintendent Lee was not in. Tibbs then asked for Superintendent Subramaniam and got him. "What can I do for you, Mr. Tibbs?" Subramaniam asked.

"Do you have a Smith and Wesson Identikit available?"

"Yes, we do."

"Could I bring Madam Motamboru this morning to make up a portrait?"

"Certainly, I'll have it set up for you whenever you like."

"We can be there in half an hour."

"We'll be ready for you."

Outside, the sun was bright in a cloudless sky, the air already warm with tropical softness. Orchard Road was swarming with traffic and the sidewalks were well filled with people. A lavishly costumed doorman waved off the first cab, which was not air conditioned, and put them into the next one, which was. Tibbs gave the address and settled back to enjoy the short ride. The huge Lucky Plaza with its hundreds of shops was already in full swing, contrasting with the dignity of Robinson's, the grande dame of department stores, safely established in its new home. In the cab Miriam reached out and took Tibbs's hand. In return he squeezed her fingers and remembered that he had to keep his mind on his work.

At the Central Police Building they were shown into the office of a man who rose quickly to greet them. He was dressed in a white Indian *dhoti*, sandals, and a white turban somewhat larger than the tighter ones commonly worn by the Sikhs. He appeared to be in his late fifties, but his full white beard made an accurate estimate difficult.

"Good morning, please sit down," he greeted them in a soft Indian voice. His English was accented and sibilant, but carefully accurate. "First of all, we must have some refreshment. What is your pleasure, madam?"

"Tea, if it is convenient," Miriam responded.

He turned to Tibbs. "And you, sir? We have tea, coffee, juices, and some other things."

Virgil sensed that to decline would be an offense, so although he had just had some, he asked for coffee. His host picked up a phone and placed the order. Then he dug into a container on his desk for some small change.

"May I be permitted—" Tibbs began, but the Indian silenced him with a shake of his head. "You are our guest here, sir. Now please tell me how I may be of assistance."

"While she was recently in Switzerland," Virgil began carefully, "Madam Motamboru was met on arrival in Geneva by a man who professed to be from the American embassy. He directed her to go immediately to Zurich, provided her with a ticket, and saw her onto a plane."

"But this man was not what he pretended to be?"

"No. The American embassy in Geneva was unaware of Mrs. Motamboru's arrival."

"Excuse my question, Mr. Tibbs, but is it possible that it was someone from another branch of your government who had not advised the embassy of his presence?"

"I considered that, sir, but his subsequent actions would indicate otherwise."

"I see. Please proceed."

A rap on the door announced the very prompt arrival of the catering service. Miriam received tea, Tibbs his coffee, and a glass of a milky liquid was set in front of the Indian policeman. Tibbs still did not know his name or his rank, but his presence in a private office at police head-quarters vouched for his reliability.

"This same man came early in the morning the following day to see Miriam at her hotel."

The heavily bearded face did not conceal a pair of penetratingly intelligent eyes. "Allow me to understand, Mr. Tibbs. The man met Madam in Geneva and dispatched her to Zurich. He called on her early the following morning, in Zurich?"

"That's right, sir."

"This is also the man, then, who passed her on, so to speak, to Singapore."

Tibbs nodded.

"And you wish to make up an Identikit portrait of this individual."

"If that can be arranged."

"It has been done; our artist is awaiting you. I regret that his English is not very good; he spent several years studying art in France before he joined us and had little opportunity to improve himself."

Miriam spoke for the first time. "I speak French," she said, "if that would be more convenient for him."

"I understand that his French is excellent; this is most fortunate. Shall we go now?"

The Indian finished his drink and rose to his feet.

Despite his unconventional garb, he led the way with dignity through an open courtyard, up an outside staircase and two additional flights inside; there was no elevator. He opened the door of a workroom and ushered in his guests.

The police artist who rose to meet them was a fairly young man of indeterminate ancestry. His features were basically Caucasian, but he showed some evidence of Oriental descent in his eyes. It was not at all marked, but it contrasted slightly with his complexion, which was on the dark side. His manner was open and cooperative, but a partial language barrier inhibited him. He seemed hesitant to speak. Then he offered, "Hello, please good morning," obviously doing his best.

Miriam gave him a relaxed, easy smile. *"Comment ça va aujourd'hui?"*

In a matter of seconds she and the artist had established a rapport. The Indian policeman nodded slightly in approval. "She is very fluent," he said.

"She took a doctorate at the Sorbonne," Tibbs told him.

"Mr. Ekivan is studying English very diligently; he is enrolled in evening classes. I think you will find him professionally competent."

With visibly increased confidence the artist set up the Identikit and began to lay out an array of facial contours. Miriam studied them and narrowed the choice down to two. On the first of the outlines the artist next began to lay out eye patterns, virtual photographs of varying eye shapes carefully graded in successive steps. This time after a little study Miriam was able to make a single selection.

Noses followed, then lips, ears, and hair. Under the artist's deft fingers the picture began to grow. Twice Miriam stopped him to change a choice she had made. When the whole thing was finished, in less then ten minutes, she viewed the composite portrait objectively and with effortless ease in French suggested some very minor changes. When they had been made, she nodded her approval. On the make-up board there was a near photograph of a man without sharply distinguishing features, but clearly identifiable.

"I have seen the Identikit used many times," Tibbs said to his host, "but your man is outstanding."

"It is because Madam's descriptions were so clear and accurate," the Indian answered. "I could tell that without understanding the words being spoken."

Twenty minutes later Tibbs escorted Miriam out of the

headquarters building and lined up at the cab stop. When it was their turn he put her inside and directed the driver to the American embassy. "Now," he said, "I believe we're going to start getting some answers."

Lee Kong Ho knew that after the racking night he had just put in, he would be no good at all until he had had some rest. He went home, called his office to say that he would be in around noon, and hit the sheets. Four hours later he got up again, knowing that he had to go to work whether he felt like it or not.

He ate a hasty meal and then headed for the Central Police Building on Robinson Road. He was in the act of sitting down behind his desk when a youthful subordinate came in with a message. "Mr. Quek Jew Kiang has been most anxious to reach you. He is head of security at the Leong Shipyards. He would not give any information over the telephone, but he asks that you see him as soon as possible. He believes that he has information that may break the Tan case."

Lee felt a fresh surge of energy run through his body. "Call him immediately," he directed, "and tell him that I'm on my way."

Chapter Fifteen

The drive to the Leong Shipyards did not take Lee Kong Ho more than fifteen minutes. During that time a multitude of ideas churned through his mind. One of them was an awareness that he had not yet given close attention to the details of engineer Tan's work. Now that job was apparently going to be done for him. All help would be gratefully received, but he was inwardly humiliated to have been caught asleep that way.

The shipyard was a huge and busy place engulfed in an aura of noise. There was hammering, the sound of powerful engines running, the hard clatter of rivets being driven, the banging of metallic parts being brought together, the hissing of steam hoses, and a cacophony of other industrial sounds that all blended into a composite din. Lee parked his car and went to see the man who might be able to help him solve the Tan case. The deaths of the two children, and the attempt on the third, haunted him night and day; Marley's ghost would not have found room to wedge itself in.

Lee's police credentials got him quickly through the gate and into the building where the security detail was housed. The head of the department, Quek Jew Kiang, was waiting for him when he came in the door. The security chief was an older man who had once served in the police in northern China. After his forced retirement he had followed in the footsteps of a great many police officers throughout the world and had gone into security work. At the shipyard his ability to speak the northern dialects had been partially responsible for his advancement to his present position. His hair was definitely thinning and his abdomen was larger than he would have liked, but within limits he kept himself in condition. He was, after all, an executive now and a department head.

After the inevitable offer of tea and Lee's polite refusal, the two men got down to business.

"As you know," Quek began, "I've made available to you all of our records concerning Engineer Tan. Everything he has ever done here, so far, has been to his credit. He is not only a good engineer, he is highly conscientious and a model of deportment."

"I know," Lee said a little abruptly. He was very anxious for Quek to come to the point.

"When the Tan case broke, I realized at once that Tan himself was a prime suspect, despite his good reputation. Then I learned that he had been cleared. However, I wondered if something connected with his work might be the cause of the dreadful murders—some enemy he did not even know he had."

"Very astute thinking," Lee said, principally to keep the ball rolling.

"So I planted one of my own men in the labor group working under Tan's direction."

Lee lifted an eyebrow. "How did you manage that?" he asked.

"There was a very good worker in the sector. I had him promoted to a better job; that created the opening. Inside of a week my man was able to report some very interesting information."

"You hold me spellbound," Lee said.

"You remember the ship sinkings, Lee, when in each case the whole crew was in on the scam?"

"Very well indeed."

"On checking the personnel records, I learned that the men in Tan's work force had all carefully managed to get themselves assigned under him. When we needed a certain type of skill, a man with just those qualifications came forward at the right moment. I have now determined that they all belong to the same secret society."

"Then you can roast them alive and they won't talk," Lee said.

"True, but when my man came into their little group, they had no choice but to cut him into their plans. Of course he agreed to cooperate—providing he got his share. That was agreed to."

"And, please, what were their plans?" It was rude to ask that, especially between Chinese, but Lee was becoming increasingly impatient.

"Tan is designing the ducts for part of the air-conditioning system of a new ship. Naturally they were laid out to fit closely with other plumbing and conduits. The men doing the actual work proposed a deal: they wanted him to add a dummy duct in one section, one that would provide almost five square meters of secret storage space. Even the most careful inspection of the ship would probably not reveal that an unnecessary duct had been added to an already complicated maze of piping."

"It would show on the plans."

"No. All Lee had to do was to allow enough room on his design. With the extra duct in place it would pass as a very economical use of space, if anyone cared to look."

"Did Tan cooperate?"

"No, he refused. My man discovered that. But Lee, have you any idea how much profit could be realized by having a virtually foolproof hiding space on that ship?"

"It would depend on the routes the vessel is going to ply."

Quek took rich satisfaction in supplying the answer. "Basically Bangkok, Sri Lanka, Malaysia, Hong Kong—and the United States west coast."

Lee thought that one over very carefully. "The smugglers would have to be skilled in secret loading and unloading."

Quek lit a cigarette. "If they had the space for it," he said, "they could load the Reclining Buddha." Lee knew he meant the immense one in Bangkok, one of the great sights of that exotic city.

"What you are telling me," Lee began slowly, "is that Tan wouldn't go along. So the pressure was applied. But would they go as far as to start killing his children?"

Quek leaned back in his chair and looked, figuratively, into the past. "Kong Ho, do you remember the American who put a bomb on an airplane to kill everyone on board, including his mother, for her insurance money?"

"That was a long time ago," Lee said.

"How about the man who set his little son on fire, again for insurance money?"

Lee rubbed his hands across his face. "Don't remind me of such horrors," he said. "I know there are people who will do anything for money. And although Tan is not a secret society member, he could still be put under terrible pressure."

Quek slowly nodded. "Think of the immense profits from just five cubic meters of space, if it were filled with 999 morphine blocks, cocaine, hashish—even expensive watches, cameras, and jewelry."

"With a hiding place that secure," Lee added as he thought, "if too close a watch were being kept on the ship, the secret cargo could be left alone and unloaded at another port of call—or even on the next voyage."

"Quite true."

Lee was thinking. "How much harm would it do," he asked, "to allow the gang to go ahead and install the dummy conduit before we nab them?"

"We might even allow them to load it," Quek suggested.

It was silent then for several seconds. "I will have to talk with my superiors," Lee said finally. "You advise your management—very discreetly. Then we'll make a decision."

"I have already spoken with my management," Quek replied. "They are willing to do whatever is necessary to catch this gang blood-handed."

"That's red-handed," Lee told him, "but you have the right idea. It's possible we could seize millions in contraband."

"And you will become a full superintendent."

"Never mind that. I have been in New York: I saw there what hard dope does to people. That is enough for me."

"Let us meet again tomorrow, at some quiet place," Quek said.

"By all means," Lee agreed.

From a phone booth in the lobby of the Crossroads, Virgil Tibbs called the American embassy and asked to speak to Jason Myers. When he had his man on the line, he wasted no time in preliminaries. "I have a picture to show you," he said.

"Bring it."

"There's a lady with me."

"Fine."

Virgil hung up with the knowledge that news travels fast in Singapore; it had been no surprise to Jack Myers that Miriam Motamboru was out of jail and in his company. He collected Miriam and five minutes later was in a cab head-ing down past the Raffles Hotel, a Singapore national monument. His mind was so firmly locked onto the work he was doing, he was hardly aware of her presence beside him. So much hinged on what he might be able to learn within the next few minutes.

At the embassy a Chinese girl who spoke flawless English took them to Myers's office and tapped discreetly on the door. Then she opened it and showed them inside.

Before Tibbs could open his mouth to perform introductions, Myers came forward and took over. "Mrs. Motamboru," he said. "I'm Jack Myers. Delighted to meet you. Your reputation for beauty is well founded."

"You should have seen me in jail," Miriam answered.

Tibbs strongly suspected that Jack's sudden cordial manner was an act, one designed to put the unsuspecting subject at her ease. The man was a pro, and a very smooth one when he chose.

"I understand you have a picture to show me," Myers said.

Tibbs produced it and handed it over. Jack looked at it for a moment, then put it down on his desk. "It's very good," he said. "I take it, Mrs. Motamboru, this is the man who intercepted you in Switzerland and sent you here."

Miriam was equally quick off the mark. "You recognized him," she said.

"I didn't say that," Myers countered.

"No, but you said that the picture was very good. That implies recognition."

"Yes," Myers conceded, "it does." He dropped all pretense of a social call and assumed a much more serious tone. "Mrs. Motamboru, on the instructions of my superiors, I'm going to put you in the picture—to a degree. But it must be on a basis of complete secrecy."

"Would you like me to leave?" Tibbs asked.

Myers shook his head. "You've been cleared for this," he said, "but thanks anyway." He turned back to Miriam.

131

"I don't know all of the details yet," he began. "For one thing, I'm not sure why Singapore was selected—I can only guess. It does have the right kind of amenities, but so do Hong Kong, Tokyo, Manila, and some other places. However, Singapore also has a strict system of justice that's efficiently administered."

"And," Miriam added, "the death penalty—by hanging."

"I wasn't going to mention that," Myers said, "but it might have been a factor."

Miriam folded her hands in her lap. "Please tell me about the man in the picture," she said.

"He has several names," Myers said. "His real one is Geoffrey Ebelman. He was born in England, raised in America. He's a Russian agent: very clever and very deadly."

"I never questioned that he was an American diplomat," Miriam admitted. "I should have known better."

"According to what I'm told, he carries very convincing credentials: I know where they're made. The fact that he was put in barefaced, as we say, indicates how important they felt it was to get you permanently out of the way. If they could discredit you completely . . ."

"I understand," Miriam said. "Even if I didn't hang as a convicted murderess, I would be destroyed politically."

"They would consider that worth exposing one of their top agents," Myers added.

Miriam was fully self possessed. "Do you think, Mr. Meyers, now that I'm free, that they'll try again?"

Myers's features tightened until there were sharp lines across his brow. "That's a hard question for me to answer," he said, picking his words. "The best I can do right now is suggest that you stay as close to Virgil as you can. Whatever else, don't go off to any places on your own, even in Singapore."

Chapter Sixteen

As soon as his guests had left the embassy, Jack Myers made a telephone call to Central Police Headquarters. He was put through to Superintendent Vashi Dalwani, who happened to be a particularly good friend of his. "Are you at liberty?" Myers asked.

"Yes," Dalwani answered.

"Are there any dark clouds on the horizon?"

"I am confident there are none, but I will take precautions."

"Good." With that Jack hung up.

When he reached the police building he ducked quickly through the lobby and into the safety of Dalwani's office. As he shut the door behind him, Dalwani rose in greeting. "I have ordered cold beer," he said.

Myers sat down without ceremony. "You entertained our friend Mr. Tibbs this morning," he began.

The Indian nodded. "And the lady. Ekivan made up an Identikit portrait for them. Would you like to see it?"

"I already have." He stopped when the door opened and a middle-aged Chinese woman with a pronounced waddle came in with a bottle of very cold beer and another of the milky drinks that Dalwani preferred. The Indian paid her and watched her out the door.

"I have some questions," Myers said.

"By all means."

"Were you present when the portrait was made up?"

"Yes, of course."

"Your impression." Myers reached for the beer and took a welcome drink.

"I was at a disadvantage," Dalwani said. "Ekivan's English is poor, but he speaks fluent French. He and Madam conversed in that language."

"Since it is very difficult for a witness to fool an experienced Identikit operator, I'd like to know Ekivan's opinion."

Dalwani nodded. "His English, as I said, is limited. You don't speak Bengali, so I asked him for you. He's convinced that Madam's directions were genuine."

"Do you agree?"

"Yes. I was watching her very closely, and Tibbs as well. I'm sure she hadn't been coached."

Myers had some more beer. "I recognized the portrait as soon as I saw it. It's a good job."

"I thought so too," Dalwani agreed. "Madam made one or two small mistakes as it was being built, but she corrected them very quickly. She was hardly a third of the way through when I recognized the subject."

Myers drank the last of his beer. As he did so his host touched a bell push hidden by a pile of papers on his desk. "A very dangerous man," Dalwani added. "Unfortunately, he's not where we can lay our hands on him."

The plump Chinese woman, who must have been just outside, came in with a fresh bottle of beer. She delivered it to Myers and went out again, apparently oblivious to everything else.

"What are your thoughts?" Myers asked.

"In my judgment, two things are gained. Madam's story about her adventure in Switzerland is now supported." The Indian leaned forward slightly, but did not change his calm, even manner. "How many pictures of Ebelman have you seen?" he asked.

Myers thought briefly before he gave a quick nod. "Good point," he said. "The few we have are surveillance photographs, none good enough to have been used to fake the Identikit portrait. Your second point?"

"With him arranging matters, I can now believe that Madam was somehow expertly framed. Either that or she's guilty—take your choice."

"Tibbs claims he can prove her innocent," Myers said.

"Your Mr. Tibbs does not allow grass to grow beneath his feet. The first thing he did after Madam was released was to bring her here to do the Identikit portrait. I made note of that. He may relieve us of a major embarrassment. I wish he were ours."

"What would you do if he were?"

"I would assign him to the Tan killings. It is the worst case we have had in years."

In the privacy of his office Deputy Commissioner Arthur Sim was taking a report from Sergeant Ng, one of the best investigators on his personal staff. The report was verbal because Sim wanted nothing in writing at that stage of the game.

"As soon as she was released," Ng said, "she went directly to the hotel. The manager had already arranged for her bags to be sent up. He also had Mr. Tibbs's things moved into the second bedroom, which is at the opposite side of the suite."

"He would be careful to keep up appearances," Sim commented.

"Mr. Tibbs and Madam had dinner with Mr. Chang, at his invitation, in the top-floor dining room. Tibbs told the maître d' it was one of the finest meals of his life."

"A diplomatic thing for him to say, and also probably

135

true. The food is magnificent and the service is splendid. So are the prices."

"It is not for poor policemen—of the lower ranks," Ng hastily added. "Anyhow, Tibbs and Madam did not leave the hotel that evening. They danced together in the cocktail lounge, then retired to their suite. Security had them covered at all times, but there were no incidents."

"Good enough," Sim commented.

"In the morning, after they had left the hotel, I spoke with Madam Ling, the housekeeper. She has thirteen years' experience at her job."

"She wouldn't be assigned to the diplomatic floor without it," Sim said.

"Yes, sir. With Madam Ling I inspected the suite. It is definite that the lady slept in her bedroom and Tibbs in his. Madam Ling would not be fooled by a casually rumpled bed."

"That's good to know, but we don't need to intrude into matters that aren't our concern. Carry on. If they separate, stay with the lady. After seeing that Identikit portrait, I don't want her left unprotected for a moment."

"Understood," Ng said. "I'll pass your instructions to the other members of the detail."

Assistant Superintendent Lee took the first opportunity to confer with Inspector Ajit Singh, the head of the Organized Crime Division. The tall Sikh listened intently as Lee described his conversation at the Leong Shipyards.

"A secret hiding place aboard ship is one of the oldest ideas in the world," the inspector said, "but this may be a new twist. The profits from using that much secure space could be enormous. Loading it here would not be hard, but unloading in the United States is another matter."

"Possibly not," Lee said, "if the members of the society could secure berths as part of the ship's crew. Then the same group could both load and unload the contraband."

Singh was forced to agree. "The ship's officers would have to be in on the deal. It would be safe for them, because they could always plead ignorance of the whole thing."

"What is your opinion?" Lee asked. "We can nail them after the construction is completed, or wait until the contraband is loaded."

"Wait until it is loaded and the ship is ready to sail. We might even stop her in the harbor on the way out; that would guarantee less interference."

"A good idea," Lee said.

A twelve-man detail drawn from the Special Enforcement Team was keeping a protective net over Madam Wee and the two surviving Tan children. In addition W.P.C. Ooi was assigned to stay with the family as a visible presence. The child that had been poisoned remained under guard in the hospital. Her brother, the only Tan child that had not been attacked, was expertly shadowed every hour of the waking day and watched over while he slept.

Because the three previous incidents had taken three different forms, no one knew what to expect. Tan himself continued to go to work, aware that the shipyard security was keeping very close watch over him. The situation was tense and as the hours ticked away, it became increasingly so.

At the Central Police Building, Lee took a call on his private line from Tibbs. "If possible," Virgil said, "I'd like to talk to the head of your Intelligence Division. That is, if you think he will tell me anything at all."

"He might. The word has come down from on high to give you reasonable help, if possible." His voice hardened a little. "Why in hell didn't you tell me that you were going to have Mrs. Motamboru do an Identikit? Now I've got egg all over my face."

"I tried to call you, but you weren't in. I left a message."

"Next time, Virgil, wait until we've communicated. As sure as God made little red apples, Arthur Sim is going to ask me why I didn't think of that. If I could have been with you, it would have saved my face."

"What can I say?" Tibbs asked. "Please forgive me."

"I'll see what I can do for you with Intelligence." With that Lee hung up.

He called back ten minutes later, somewhat cooled down. "I'm sorry I lit into you, Virgil," he said. "You did try to call me. Superintendent Jurong, who's head of Intelligence, is expecting your visit. Anytime today will be all right."

Forty minutes later Tibbs presented himself at the Intelligence Division. As soon as he entered the outer office, he was greeted by name and taken to see the superintendent in change.

"My name is Jurong," his host said. "I'm delighted you've come to visit us. What would you enjoy?"

He was a slender, somewhat dark-skinned man who wore his thick black hair parted high on his head. Apart from a somewhat sharp nose, his features were regular with no hint of any particular ancestry. There was a sense of understanding in his dark brown eyes, but they also hinted at a barrier behind which no one could trespass.

"Nothing, thank you," Virgil answered.

"I'm sorry, Mr. Tibbs, that our building isn't air conditioned. The new one will be, but we will have to wait awhile. How may I help you?"

"I'd appreciate knowing whatever you can tell me, if anything, about a Geoffrey Ebelman, reputed to be a Russian agent."

Jurong smiled. It was pleasant enough, but it gave nothing whatever away.

"I so admire the American talent for coming right to the point," he said. "But why do you not ask your embassy people for this information?"

Tibbs spoke carefully. "Because, sir, by training and experience I naturally turn first to a police organization, especially one that has an Intelligence Division. If my request is improper, I understand perfectly."

"Mr. Tibbs, as you know very well, we are instructed to cooperate with you as much as we feel able. However, we know very little about this man. To the best of my knowledge, he has never been in Singapore."

"There is a man operating here who told Madam Motamboru his name was John Smith," Tibbs said. "The only information I have, apart from a general description, is that he is probably a non-British European."

Jurong showed a modicum of interest. "How did you determine that?"

"Mrs. Motamboru told me that when this man called on her, he spoke English 'without a trace of an accent.' "

"You mean, she recognized that it was not his native tongue."

"Yes, without realizing it."

"A question, Mr. Tibbs. Why, when Madam was at the Central Police Building, didn't you ask her to do a second portrait of the man who called on her. This 'John Smith'?"

"I hoped it wouldn't be necessary."

"Why?"

Tibbs laced his fingers and pressed them hard together. "According to Mrs. Motamboru's account, which I believe to be true, Smith recited exactly the same story she had been told by Ebelman in Zurich. He also gave some further reasons why she'd been routed to Singapore. This definitely proves that he's part of the same organization that used Ebelman to intercept her in Switzerland."

"I agree. Please continue."

"In your position as the Intelligence Division commander, this man Smith would obviously have received your close attention."

Jurong paused. He ran a hand across his chin as he thought, and then made a decision. "Mr. Tibbs, we believe we know who this John Smith is. That's in strict confidence. We're trying to get hold of him now. Meanwhile, let me give you a word of caution. He's a very dangerous and relentless man. He's highly skilled in armed and unarmed combat and will kill without hesitation. What will interest you particularly: he probably engineered the assassination of President Motamboru."

"Is he Russian?" Tibbs asked.

"Definitely a Russian agent; I don't know his birthplace. I'm telling you this so you won't try to go up against this man on a one-to-one basis. I know you're a superior policeman, but you're not an agent, which is a very different thing. Also, we know you're recuperating from a shooting incident."

"I have no idea where he is," Tibbs said.

"You won't find him, but he may find you. If he does, don't try to take him. He's extremely proficient, and he'll know what you intend before you do. Let us do it: we have the resources and the personnel to bring him in. Besides, you might not care for a Chinese funeral. I hope I haven't offended you."

"Of course not," Tibbs said. "You've given me a warning that could save my hide."

Jurong stood up. "I'm most happy that you called," he said.

On the way out of the lobby Tibbs was intercepted by the desk and handed a message.

Please call Assistant Superintendent Lee immediately.

As soon as he had read it, a telephone was set on the counter for him to use. He dialed and got Lee on the first ring.

"Have you been to the Shangri-La yet?" Lee asked.

"No, I haven't."

"There is a noontime Western-style buffet that's exceptional. Meet me by the waterfall as soon as you can."

"Is it urgent?"

"Yes, Virgil, come now."

"I'm on my way."

"See you soon." Lee hung up.

The hotel had extensive, lavishly landscaped grounds that made it something of an island in the center of busy Singapore. A large cascading waterfall accentuated an exotic tropical setting that contrasted with the huge lobby and elegant shops that lay just inside. The dining room to which Lee led the way was isolated in air-conditioned quiet. Long tables had been set out, with a wide variety of entrées and salads on one, desserts on another, and beverages on a third. There was a smaller one exclusively for the serving of various kinds of ice cream.

Plate in hand, Tibbs went down the line and did his best to restrain himself. At the beverage service a very pretty Chinese girl handed him a glass of iced tea at his request. She gave him a warm smile before he turned to follow Lee to a corner table. The dining room was moderately full, but all the tables were well separated throughout the large room, giving ample privacy to everyone.

When they were seated, Lee asked an unexpected question. "Virgil, what's on your mind at this moment?"

"The smile I got from the young lady at the beverage table. She made me feel as though we might become friends someday."

"In Singapore, very easily," Lee said. "We've got a pretty good city here, despite the fact that all the shows are censored. Even *Playboy* magazine isn't allowed."

After ice water had been served and the meal begun, Lee got down to business.

"First off, Virgil, I gave you a buildup before you came

here. So far you've made me look good; forget the Identikit incident. Now I want to ask you something: do you know the identity of the body found in Madam Motamburo's suite?"

"Yes," Tibbs answered. "But it wasn't in the file you gave me."

"I know. Let me fill you in. After the autopsy, the body was cremated. Shortly after that Jack Myers bought a nice blue and white Chinese vase and shipped it home to some friends. It was buried with its contents after private services. There were some official condolences."

"How do you know all this?" Tibbs asked.

"We try to keep track of what's going on. Now, there has been a development in the Tan case. For my own reasons, I want to run it past you, off the record."

As he ate, Lee supplied the details concerning the dummy duct being built into the new ship, the involvement of the secret society, and the pressures that had been applied to Engineer Tan to force his cooperation. Tibbs listened silently, eating slowly as he did so. When Lee had finished, he shook his head. "The way you tell it, it doesn't add up."

"Explain," Lee invited.

"All right. Tan is the engineer in charge of that particular area, so he's a key man in the plan."

"Yes, we realize that."

"But you told me that in every respect he's Mr. Clean. So to force his cooperation, the secret society threatened his family. Under that duress he went along and so far has kept his mouth tight shut."

"True."

"Then someone began to go after his children. Isn't it more likely that his family would be attacked if he *didn't* cooperate?"

"I saw that, of course, Virgil, but look at it this way: The society has a lot at stake here; it's a major operation that could go on for years. Now suppose that Tan told them he couldn't go along anymore, warned them that he was going to blow the whistle. Or he could have claimed that inspectors were going over all of the designs and that the dummy duct was sure to be detected. To apply more pressure to him, the society began to carry out its threats. If several people were involved, that would account for the different methods used to get at the Tan children."

Tibbs shook his head. "If inspectors go over the designs, they would do it before construction begins, so that threat is presumably in the past. And if an honorable man had been forced as far as Tan was, it's unlikely, I think, that he would then change his mind and risk the society's revenge on his family. Also, he'd have to implicate himself to a degree."

Lee remained thoughtful for a little while as he ate. "That makes sense," he said at last. "Mainly, Virgil, I wanted to bounce this off someone else. I invited you here to tip you off that we knew all about the man found dead in Madam's suite. If you see Arthur Sim again, for God's sake don't ask him why he didn't give you the word when you had lunch. I happen to know that he chose not to. You scored enough when you got her out of the can; settle for that."

"I intend to," Tibbs said. "I assumed that I couldn't dig something out in one day, on Sim's territory, that he didn't already know. Going back to the Tan case, the secret society could be attacking the Tan children, but my guess is that you've got to have to look somewhere else entirely. Unless there's something you haven't told me, as far as suspects and motive go, you're back on square one."

Chapter Seventeen

After the lunch was over, Virgil checked with the Crossroads message desk. There had been a call for him from the American embassy: he was asked to return it as soon as possible.

The girl at the embassy switchboard had been alerted. "Yes, Mr. Tibbs," she said, "one moment please."

Another female voice came on the line. It was smooth and professional. "Mr. Tibbs, Ambassador Thatcher would like to see you this afternoon. Would three o'clock be convenient?"

Tibbs glanced at his watch: it was already two-thirty. "I'll be there," he said.

He spent five minutes in a washroom adjusting his appearance, then he went down to the lobby and allowed a resplendent doorman to put him into a cab. He held out a Singapore dollar as a tip, but the man waved it aside. "My pleasure," he said.

Because of the restrictions on private cars in the city center during business hours, traffic was comparatively light. The taxi pulled up in front of the embassy at ten minutes to the hour, which suited Tibbs perfectly. Punctuality was close to a religion with him; he was never late for anything if it possibly could be avoided.

At the desk he gave his name and waited while the receptionist phoned. "Someone will be down for you right away, Mr. Tibbs," she said.

A pleasant and businesslike Indian girl almost as dark-skinned as Tibbs himself came to get him. "Please come with me," she said, and led the way inside. She guided him to a sizable corner office and indicated that he should go in. She followed and performed the introduction. "Ambassador Thatcher, Mr. Virgil Tibbs."

The two men shook hands, then the ambassador indicated an informal grouping of chairs in a corner of the office. He was suntanned and obviously very fit. He had lost most of his hair at an early age, but it did not appear to make a great deal of difference. He wore a light tan safari suit of the kind seen so much on the streets of the city.

"Thank you for coming on such short notice," the ambassador said. "I've been away, and I did want to see you as soon as I could."

"It was no problem at all," Tibbs said.

"Good. Mr. Tibbs, I think it would be prudent for me to explain to you some aspects of your mission here. Then if you have any questions, I'll try to answer them for you."

"At this point, sir, I have only one," Virgil answered. "But it can wait until later."

"How about a cold Coke, or some beer?"

"I've just had an enormous lunch. I'll pass."

"Mr. Tibbs, let me begin by saying that I know all about your protection of Mrs. Motamboru—when she was being given temporary sanctuary in Pasadena. You added to your reputation with that operation." The ambassador's tone became more careful. "I'd like this conversation to be just between ourselves."

"Understood," Virgil said.

"We're very interested in Miriam Motamboru: in her welfare, obviously, and also she was bringing some very

145

important information to us, information we very much want to have. But it's now disappeared."

"Perhaps only temporarily," Tibbs said.

The ambassador gave him a quick look. "If it were necessary, do you think you could find it?"

"I believe so," Tibbs replied.

"Now," Thatcher continued, "concerned as we are with Mrs. Motamboru, she isn't an American citizen. So we can only go so far—officially. She came here and was promptly involved in a killing. There are relatively few murders in Singapore, because the odds are better than four to one that if you kill someone here, you'll go the gallows for it."

The ambassador stopped long enough to invite comment, but Tibbs kept still.

"May I call you Virgil?"

"Please."

"Because the Straits of Malacca have tremendous economic and military importance, it would be a major coup for certain powers if they could bring Singapore into their sphere of influence. One way would be to erode confidence in the present government. That would be very difficult, but like a political party out of power in an election year, they'll use every opportunity to take potshots. I suspect that may be behind Mrs. Motamboru's present difficulties."

"I'm convinced, sir, that she was set up."

"That seems quite likely. If Singapore let her off without a satisfactory explanation, they'd raise a howl all over the Far East. They'd stretch it out like Watergate, play up the idea that she's rich and privileged and therefore immune to normal justice. That's a strong appeal to people who barely have enough to eat."

"I can understand that," Tibbs said. "I've been in that position."

The ambassador took note before he continued. "Now

146

let me explain how you fit into this. You know that when she found herself in deep trouble, Mrs. Motamboru almost desperately asked if you could be made available to help her. The Singapore people called me in and we made a deal." He shifted his position on his chair.

"The police here are very efficient and they know their job. Look at the city and you'll see the proof of that. You may have thought it a little odd when they know this jurisdiction intimately, and have excellent detectives of their own, that they let us bring in an outsider. Especially one, no matter how capable, who hadn't ever been here."

"I presumed, Mr. Thatcher, that it was to satisfy Miriam's request."

"Partly that, yes, but it was also political. The police had a strong case against Mrs. Motamboru, but they smelled a setup from the beginning. They were smart enough to keep it to themselves. The deal was simple: I agreed to try and get hold of you. Singapore agreed to give you cooperation, to take the heat off them. You see, Virgil, you could afford to succeed, but the way the cards were stacked, they could not. If you were working with them, there would be very little loss of face involved. That's important over here. And the opposition would have no ammunition whatever to shoot."

Virgil sat quietly for a few moments, then he looked up. "A question, sir: do they already have the answers and am I only spinning my wheels?"

Thatcher shook his head vigorously. "Definitely not, Virgil. The matter of the wrong body found dead in the locked hotel suite has everybody stopped. Also they've got a very tough multiple murder on their hands right now and it's taking up a lot of their available man-hours. When you came in you said you had a question."

"Yes. According to Miriam, when she came here she received a prompt call from this embassy. She called back

147

and verified it. She was told she would be contacted shortly, but she never was. Can you explain that for me?"

The ambassador leaned back and closed his eyes while he thought. It was several seconds before he replied. "Your information is correct: now do me a favor and forget it. I'll say that we didn't slip up here, but I can't go farther."

"You don't have to, sir, I can see it myself."

"Meaning what?"

"I know, Mr. Thatcher, that the dead man found in Mrs. Motamboru's suite was an American agent. Undoubtedly he had learned that something was up and asked to have a clear track."

Thatcher thought again briefly, then said, "No comment."

Virgil stood up. "Thank you for your time," he said.

As he was walking out of the lobby, he was surprised to find waiting for him the same tall, immaculately uniformed and turbanned Sikh who had met him at the airport.

"Mr. Tibbs, I am Ajit Singh," the man said. "It was my great pleasure to meet you on your arrival."

"Thank you, Inspector," Tibbs responded. "What can I do for you?"

"I was driving past when I heard you were calling here. May I offer you a ride back to your hotel?"

"If it isn't out of your way."

"Not at all, sir, not at all."

Tibbs followed Singh outside, to be met by a near blast of afternoon tropical heat. How Singh managed to remain so unaffected in his crisp uniform he could not imagine. The car was another of the blue police vehicles without markings; Singh unlocked it and opened the door for Tibbs before he got in himself. As he was starting the engine Virgil remarked, "I'm sorry to have kept you waiting for so long."

Singh dropped all pretense. "Not very long," he said.

"You noted the heat in the car. Happily it is air conditioned; we will be comfortable shortly." With notable dignity he moved into traffic and headed toward Nathan Road. "I have a message for you," he said when he was ready. "It is from Deputy Commissioner Sim. He asked that I deliver it to you in person."

"Is it of a confidential nature?" Tibbs asked.

"Yes, very. And delicate as well. There has been a development in the case of Madam Motamboru."

Tibbs drew in a deep breath, preparing himself. "Yes?" he asked.

"My apologies, sir, but I am not to divulge it to you at this time. Of course you will be advised shortly."

That was a face-restoring speech if Virgil had ever heard one. When he remained silent, Singh continued. "Deputy Commissioner Sim requests that Madam Motamboru remain in her hotel until further advised. I repeat that this is a request, just for her own safety."

"May she visit the shops in the hotel?"

"Certainly. You understand that it was quite difficult to cover her when she went shopping on Nathan Road. The crowds and all that."

The two men remained quiet for three or four blocks. The air conditioning had taken hold and the car was cooling a little. Then Singh spoke once more. "This is a precaution only, not to be taken as a house arrest. Please make that clear to Madam. The hotel has every facility, even a library. We hope she will not be inconvenienced too much."

"I would like to send Mr. Sim a return message," Tibbs said. He shaped his words into the formal Singapore pattern that was becoming familiar. "His request will be strictly observed, barring events beyond our control. Madam Motamboru is profoundly grateful to be freed from detention. She will be happy to cooperate in every possible way."

Singh bowed his head to indicate his approval. "As I said

when you arrived, Mr. Tibbs, it is a great pleasure to have you here with us."

When Tibbs entered the hotel suite, Miriam was waiting for him. She was wearing a simple orchid dress that emphasized her slender waist and very trim legs. "You look hot," she said.

"I am," Virgil answered. "Let me grab a quick shower, then I have some things to tell you."

Ten minutes later, refreshed and dressed in the lightest suit he owned, he sat down beside Miriam and delivered the message. She took it very well. "How long will it last?" she asked.

"I don't know," Tibbs answered. "I'm going to have to leave you here alone quite a bit, but security will be looking after you. I'm sure that Mr. Chang has already been notified. I'm sorry."

Miriam leaned toward him to be reassured. He held her gently, then kissed her on the cheek before he broke away. "Virgil, what does it mean?" she asked.

Tibbs decided to tell her. "It means that the man you know as John Smith is back here again. Obviously for a reason."

Miriam swallowed, then looked at him. "It means that I'm likely to be attacked again, doesn't it," she said in a calm, even voice.

"Not if I can get to him first," Tibbs replied.

Chapter Eighteen

After a brief dinner with Miriam, Virgil excused himself and went out to do some essential thinking and also to deepen his grasp and understanding of the city/nation that was Singapore. He began by taking a bus to the shoreline, where the huge harbor was comfortably filled with a wide array of ships. An American aircraft carrier was in port; she was anchored well out, away from the multitude of international freighters, the coastal traders of the South China Sea, and the many smaller vessels that were tied up at various docks.

On the sterns of many of the smaller ships he was able even in the twilight to read names that quickened his blood a little: Bali, Sumatra, Penang, Bangkok, Sidney, Auckland, Hong Kong, Manila, even Columbo. It brought home to him once more where he was, and how far away from home.

At the water's edge concealed spotlights were illuminating the white, sitting-up lion that was the symbol of Singapore. A steady stream of water poured out of the lion's mouth and arced into the harbor, an example, perhaps, of the life that flowed continuously through the tropical city.

He walked along the shoreline: open water on one side of him, towering modern high rises on the other. A pedicab went past; the driver rang his bell in hopes of picking up a fare, but Virgil waved him off.

He came to a sizable plaza dominated by a pagodalike restaurant called the Red Lantern. Scattered around it there were many girls—teenagers or perhaps somewhat older; it was hard for him to tell. He knew immediately why they were there and that as a lone man on foot what to expect. The openness with which they congregated told him that prostitution was at least tolerated in the Lion City. Then he remembered reading that it was not illegal in Singapore and never had been: only soliciting was banned. It was a sensible arrangement, particularly in a city with a large amount of marine traffic.

Very quickly a small pack of girls began to surround him, but he waved them off with a smile. Unlike many of the pros he had encountered at home, these girls seemed happy. He remembered again that he was in Asia where so many things were vastly different.

He walked on past. Half a block away he encountered a constable. "Good evening," he said.

"Good evening, sir. Can I help you?"

"Perhaps you could tell me where those girls come from," Tibbs said.

"Largely from Thailand. They are very popular, because they give good service. If you hire one for a short time, she may stay with you all evening. They are all anxious to please."

"Most of the girls come here?"

"There are two major red-light areas that are condoned, but each of the girls has to have a medical examination by the Health Department every two weeks."

"Apart from the sex, are the houses orderly?"

"Very, they would not be tolerated otherwise."

"Thank you for all that information."

"You're welcome, Mr. Tibbs."

Virgil was mildly surprised. "How did you know me, apart from the obvious?"

"Word gets around. If I hadn't known who you were, I wouldn't have talked so freely."

"I'm out getting the feel of Singapore," Virgil said. "Where should I go next?"

"Take a pedicab through Chinatown to the Raffles Hotel. Go into the big open-air bar there and have a Singapore Sling—where it was invented."

"Where do I get the pedicab?"

"Let me do that. To you the price will be several times too much."

It was only a short wait until a pedicab came past. The constable flagged it and spoke briefly with the driver. "I have explained that you are generous and will give him two Singapore dollars. As soon as you start, he will ask for more money. You are overpaying him as it is, so refuse."

"Just as you say," Tibbs answered and climbed into the man-powered vehicle. The driver rang his bell and started out, pedaling with apparent ease. He spoke no English; when he started in Chinese, Tibbs shook his head. Sadly the man gave up and continued on.

Chinatown was unlike anything that went by the same name in the States. There was no exotic decor, no wall-to-wall parade of souvenir shops and restaurants. It was an area of many small stores selling a wide variety of merchandise: bedding, electronic equipment, secondhand clothing, and almost everything except tourist items. Virgil took it all in as the pedicab rolled slowly up the street. From the second-floor windows men in undershirts peered down while children took quick looks and then abruptly disappeared. The area did not seem any more Chinese than the whole of the city, but it was characterized by the babble of merchants' voices and the haggling of the few customers who were doing business at that hour.

When the ride up one street and down another had been completed, the pedicab turned onto a main artery. The heavy traffic of the daytime was almost entirely gone, leaving the smooth streets curiously open and free. A large, three-story white wooden building came into view; the pedicab man pulled up in front of it and motioned silently that the ride was over. Knowing that he was a softy, Tibbs handed him three dollars and received a clasped hands, bowed acknowledgement in return.

The ancient, legendary Raffles lived up to its name and reputation. The lobby was small, but the famous triangular Palm Court was all that he had hoped it would be. Concealed colored lights threw shadows of the tall palm trees across the grass, while overhead a half moon advertised the tropical night. A headwaiter offered him a candlelit table under the plastic shelter, but Virgil declined. He sought and found the long bar, stepped up, and ordered a Sling. He assumed that if he had asked for anything else, the barman would have had a stroke.

He received the tall reddish drink, paid, and took it to a nearby table. A total informality pervaded the whole large open-air room: every kind of dress was to be seen from the very formal to the completely casual. In the far corner a small company was presenting some Malay dances. Gathered in front of the stage, two groups were being entertained as part of a package tour.

When he had finished his drink and taken a regular taxi back to the Crossroads, he wondered if he had made himself visible enough. In a strange city of more than two million he could not hope to find the man who called himself John Smith, but that hardened professional could quite easily find him. If he did, despite his recent injuries, Tibbs felt that he was ready for him.

Ordinarily Assistant Superintendent Lee did not have enough rank to entitle him to a private interview with the deputy commissioner, but he had been summoned and had responded as quickly as he had been able. When Arthur Sim received him in a pleasant manner and invited him to sit down, Lee made a supreme effort not to let his relief show on his face.

Sim wasted no time. "I called you in because there's a question you may be able to answer. You are handling the Tan murder case and you're a personal friend of our distinguished American visitor."

"Yes, sir," Lee said.

"Before I ask my question, are you reasonably aware of what Tibbs is doing?"

"I believe so, sir. I can't say he's confided in me, but I have no feeling either that he's holding out."

"That isn't quite what I meant. Are you current on the progress of his investigation?"

Lee was careful. "To a degree, sir."

"Incidently, do you know if he has any special training in unarmed combat, more than the usual police skills?"

Lee could answer that without hesitation. "Yes, sir, very much so. He holds a third-degree black belt in karate. He's spent many years studying with Nishiyama, who's number one in the world. He also holds the black belt in aikido, a very advanced art."

The deputy commissioner considered that information. "I now understand why Mr. Tibbs has been taking evening walks, making himself visible on the tourist routes."

Lee deliberately changed the subject. "You wanted to ask me a question, sir."

"Yes, I did. Can you think of any good way to invite your friend to spend some of his valuable time assisting you in the Tan murders investigation?"

Lee was surprised. "Pardon me, sir, but I understood that I was to keep him out of our hair. Most of our homicide people definitely don't want him around."

"I know, but I have my reasons."

155

Lee thought for a moment. "Then, sir, I could invite him to study our methods. That way any loss of face would be avoided."

Sim was clearly pleased. "That's a good suggestion," he said. "Furthermore, if I read Tibbs correctly, he will understand without our having to draw pictures for him."

"Is he cleared for confidential access?"

"Yes. His government trusts him, and Mr. Thatcher told me that he carries a fairly high-level clearance."

Lee felt that he had time for one more question. "What level would you suggest for him, as a matter of protocol?"

"Why don't you regard him as a colleague. That seems appropriate."

Lee got up. "I'll pass the word," he said.

In the morning Tibbs had breakfast with Miriam, then he went to work. He walked up and down the hotel corridor outside the suite, using the sweep second hand of his watch. He paced off some careful measurements.

The maids were already at work on the floor. He was unable to talk to them—they spoke only Cantonese—but he had already read their statements in the file he had been given. He was again grateful that English was the official language of the Singapore Police. When one of the maids began vacuuming the corridor, he stood back and watched her, as though he had nothing else to do. The woman kept on with her work, unaware that her movements were being accurately timed to the second.

When he had done that, Tibbs gave his attention to the maid who was doing up the rooms. He examined her cart without touching anything and smiled at her when she moved from one suite to the next. He watched her as she picked up her supplies and came back with the used bedsheets and towels. Neither of the maids cared for his inspection, but they tolerated him because he was presumably a guest on the diplomatic floor. Security was not their business; they were looking forward to the midmorning break and a chance to exchange hotel gossip over tea. There was a Japanese film star who had two rooms, on different floors, with a girl in each one. They could hardly wait for the intimate details the maids on those floors would be able to give.

When Tibbs had gathered all the data that he needed, he went to the lobby phone and asked for an appointment.

The chief of security for the Crossroads Hotel was a six-foot-two, sandy-haired Australian who kept himself in condition. His abdomen was hard and flat, his complexion well tanned by the tropical sun. He received Tibbs in his comfortable, but not lavish, office, sat back, and asked what he could do for his visitor.

Virgil made himself equally comfortable. "Is there anything about what I'm doing here that you don't already know?" he asked.

"I don't think so," the Australian, whose name was Millbrae, answered.

"I propose, then, that we work together," Tibbs said. "The sooner this is all cleared up, the better it'll be for the hotel."

"Agreed," Millbrae said. "I've been expecting you before now."

"I like to get my ducks in a row before I start shooting, Mr. Millbrae."

"Tom."

"Virgil. I've done my groundwork; now I want to untangle the matter of the wrong body in Miriam Motamboru's suite."

"Think you can do it?" There was no hostility in his voice, only a moderate curiosity.

"With your help, perhaps."

Millbrae sat up straighter in his chair. "Tell me what you'd like," he said.

"I'd like to talk to the man who took the first visitor up to the suite."

"Easy. Mind if I sit in?"

"Of course not; it's your hotel."

"I wish to hell it was." Millbrae punched a button on his telephone. "Gene to the office," he said, and hung up.

Tibbs sat quietly, waiting, until a well-groomed young American came in. "Gene Knight, Virgil Tibbs," Millbrae said. "Sit down, Gene."

The young man sat. His manner, plus his job, told Tibbs at once that he was an ex-policeman. "How long were you on?" Virgil asked.

"Four years. Then I busted the mayor's daughter for coke and made it stick. So now I'm here."

"On the day that Mrs. Motamboru was arrested, you took a visitor up to her suite."

"Right. I stayed with her until she told me I could leave. Then I waited outside until I got a call on my beeper."

"And you left."

"It was a judgment call. Everything seemed okay where I was, and the call meant that I was needed somewhere else."

"That's also policy," Millbrae added. "We don't beep someone on an assignment unless there's a real need. Gene could have refused if he'd had any reason to expect trouble where he was."

"When you responded," Virgil continued, "was it a bona fide call?"

"Yes, absolutely." He stopped and looked at Millbrae.

"We had a mess in one of the rooms," the Australian said. "Man beating his wife; she caught him molesting their daughter. That's confidential."

"I don't like coincidences," Tibbs said, "but that sounds genuine."

"It was. In a hotel this size, we're kept pretty busy."

"How long were you tied up?" Virgil asked Knight.

"About forty minutes. It took that long to get them packed, checked out, and in a cab."

"Were the police notified?"

"Not this time," Millbrae answered. "Most felonies we detain the suspects and call the S.P.D. We have a couple of holding rooms. This time is was my decision to settle for getting them off the premises."

Tibbs opened his briefcase and took out the morgue photographs. He handed the top one to Knight. "Is this the man you showed up to see Mrs. Motamboru?" he asked.

The young man looked at it and shook his head. "Definitely not," he said.

"You understand that's a post mortem shot."

"Of course, but it isn't the same man. I can testify to it."

"All right," Tibbs said. "It's now established that there *were* two men in Mrs. Motamboru's suite, the one you showed up, and this one who was found there."

"Which backs her story," Millbrae said. "There must be a helluva conspiracy somewhere here."

"I doubt it," Virgil answered. "I think there was a break and the killer took advantage of it. For one thing, there wasn't time to work out any elaborate scheme, and the housemaids check out in the clear."

"True," Millbrae agreed.

"If you want to come up to the suite now," Tibbs said, "I think I can show you how it was done."

Chapter Nineteen

As the three men rode up in the elevator, Millbrae offered some information. "The twenty-second floor is a diplomatic area, used for major VIPs, heads of state, important government officials, and some celebrities. No rock bands. It's mostly all suites, some rooms for secretaries and other support personnel."

"With special security precautions," Tibbs added.

"Yes, of course. No bugging or anything like that, but the floor can be sealed off very quickly. One signal from the reception desk, the manager's office, the assistant manager's station in the lobby, or my office will lock all the fire access doors from the stairwells on that floor and the elevators will bypass it. If an elevator is open on the twenty-second, it will close and won't move until the all clear."

"Is there extra soundproofing?" Tibbs asked.

"Yes," Millbrae answered as the car stopped and the doors opened. "And some other precautions. People can't get through the air-conditioning ducts, for example. Now what can you show me?"

Virgil walked a short distance from the elevator bank toward Miriam's suite and then stopped. He turned to Gene Knight. "Think very carefully about this," he said. "When you brought the first visitor up to Mrs. Motamboru's suite, did you see the maid vacuuming the rug?"

"Yes, I did," Knight answered.

"Please show me exactly where she was, as closely as you can remember."

Knight walked twenty feet past Tibbs and then stopped. "About here," he said.

"Was she facing you?"

"No, she was working her way toward the suite, away from the elevators."

Virgil nodded. "Good. Did you see the other maid?"

"Not that I remember. I did see her cart; I'm sure of that."

Tibbs turned to Millbrae. "What about the employees assigned to this floor?" he asked.

"Hand-picked," Millbrae replied. "The maids are the best we have."

"So they can be expected to do careful, conscientious work."

"Absolutely. Otherwise, out they go."

"Do you know about that man found dead in the suite?"

"I know. So does Gene."

"All right," Tibbs said. "I'm going to lay out a scenario for you. Gene, you arrived on this floor with a man we'll call John Smith. That's the name he gave Mrs. Motamboru, by the way. Did you speak with him at all?"

"Only briefly."

"Did you notice anything?"

"No, I'm afraid not."

"Could you guess what part of the country he might be from?"

"He didn't have any particular accent. His voice was flat: no expression in it at all."

"A cold fish."

"Not exactly. I've been over this a lot in my mind. He

161

could have been a European, damn good in English he'd learned by the book."

Tibbs showed no reaction to that. "You got off the elevator with Smith. Since you were showing him to the suite, you went first."

"Right."

"You passed the maid who was vacuuming. Did you speak to her?"

"No. I probably couldn't. Most of them are Cantonese."

"When you reached the door of the suite, did you knock or ring the bell?"

"I knocked. We were expected."

"Mrs. Motamboru opened the door?"

"Yes."

"Did you go inside with Smith?"

"That's required. To make sure the guest is welcome and okay."

"How long did you stay?"

"About two minutes, until I was told everything was all right. Then I left the suite and waited outside."

Virgil led the way to the door of the suite and stopped there. "Show me where you were standing," he said.

"Almost where you are."

"And the maid with the vacuum?"

"About twenty feet down the hall—toward the elevators."

"How about the other maid?"

"Her cart was beside the door of the next suite. I remember that clearly."

"How soon after that did your beeper go off?"

"Not very long. I made the decision to respond and ran to the elevator. There was a car unloading one man, and I jumped into it."

"The man who was later found dead?"

"I don't know; I didn't really look at him."

162

"One more question: how was Smith dressed?"

"Sports outfit: dark slacks, light shirt and tie, tan jacket."

"All right," Tibbs said. "Let's go inside the suite where we can talk comfortably." He tapped on the door, then inserted his key and led the way inside.

Miriam was waiting for him. Virgil introduced the security men and then suggested that everyone sit down. Miriam offered to send for refreshments, but both Millbrae and Knight declined.

Virgil was the first to speak. "Has the Singapore Police Department filled you in on this?" he asked.

"Yes," Millbrae answered. "We know that when Mrs. Motamboru arrived here, she was carrying a package sent by her husband to your president. The KGB wanted to intercept it, and destroy her in the process. They told us that Smith is a Russian agent who's considered extremely dangerous. We're being kept current on a need-to-know basis."

At that point there was a knock on the door. Millbrae opened it and found Assistant Superintendent Lee on the other side. "May I come in?" he asked.

Lee joined the party and sat down in a carefully casual manner. "I've just learned that my friend Virgil called on you, Tom, and that you sent for the man who showed Smith up to this suite. Then the three of you came up here. Conclusion: Virgil is going to tell us how the wrong body got into this room despite reliable witnesses in the hallway. I don't want to miss that."

Millbrae turned to his young assistant. "Gene, you'd better cover the office until this meeting is over." Without comment, Knight got up and left.

"Would you like me to go also?" Miriam asked.

"Of course not," Lee replied. "Have I missed anything vital?"

"No," Virgil answered. "You timed it perfectly. Now back

to cases. As soon as Miriam arrived here, she put the document she was carrying in the hotel vault. But not in the usual way. She saw the manager, Mr. Chang, and asked for special protection for what she was carrying. Mr. Chang personally took care of it. There's no way that Smith could have known that. It was a private conversation, and Chang's discretion isn't in doubt."

"Who did know about this?" Lee asked.

Miriam answered him. "Mr. Chang, myself, and I told Virgil. No one else."

"She didn't openly put anything in the vault," Tibbs continued. "I don't know how much information the hotel will give out concerning who uses that facility."

"None," Millbrae answered, "but a resourceful person could probably find out. One way would be to ask the vault personnel if they had *seen* Mrs. Motamboru. That's an innocent-sounding question, and since she has a distinctive appearance—being unusually attractive," he added quickly, "she would be remembered."

"It was after this, while Miriam was being detained, that her lock box was opened and found to be empty," Tibbs pointed out. "Now, any apparent violation of the security of the vault would be a very hard thing to keep under wraps."

"It did leak," Millbrae admitted. "I don't know how, but I got a call from one of the papers about it. I questioned our people immediately, from all three shifts.

"With what result?" Virgil asked.

"I never thought for a moment that the vault had been breached. It's virtually impossible. And no entry could have been made without leaving some evidence behind. I checked for a possible mistake. If I had known that Mr. Chang had handled the matter, I could have saved a lot of time and effort."

"Let me make a point," Tibbs said. "If he didn't confide in you, it wasn't for any lack of trust."

"He wanted me to go through the motions," Millbrae suggested.

"Yes, and not for the drill. Just in case someone was interested."

Millbrae considered that.

"Clearly Smith was sent here to Singapore to deal with Miriam and get that package, either or both if he could," Tibbs said. "Suppose he learned that Miriam hadn't been to the vault. Tom, you said that's possible."

"Then he'd assume I was stupid enough to keep the package either with me or in this room," Miriam said.

"There are many people who are dangerously overconfident," Virgil added. "They often say, 'I can take care of myself,' when they can't.

"Now some things begin to line up. We know that Smith was after Miriam: he attacked her right here. We know his motive: he wanted the package he believed was somewhere in the suite. He took her unawares with a chancery chokehold and, when she was out, gave her a shot where it wouldn't show and went to work."

"I'll buy it so far," Lee said.

"Shortly after Miriam arrived here, she got a call from the American embassy. The American intelligence people knew she was coming, and probably why. You know the identity of the man found dead here. He'd been operating in Bakara, obviously under cover, because Miriam didn't recognize him when she saw his body. His being so promptly on the scene means he'd been covering her. He was probably on the same flight."

"I happen to know that's true," Lee said.

"Now the sequence of events. Miriam had been attacked and was unconscious. 'Smith' began an intensive search of the suite. One of the first things he would find was her gun in the nightstand. He may have had one himself, but from his known history, a knife would be more likely.

165

"The American who was covering Miriam was in the hotel, probably as a registered guest."

"He was," Milbrae contributed.

"Knowing his job," Tibbs continued, "he knew when Miriam had a visitor. After a few minutes he walked past the suite, just to be sure that everything was all right. When he saw there was no security man outside, he knocked on the door."

"With the old excuse ready that he had made a mistake," Millbrae commented.

"Smith was in the suite," Tibbs went on. "He'd found the gun, but was still searching, otherwise he would have left."

Virgil paused and consciously took a deep breath. When he had let it out, he continued. "Now about the maids. Two of them were working close by. One was making up the rooms. She had a cart with her supplies and a large bag to hold soiled linen and towels. Almost all of her work was inside the rooms. Tom mentioned on the way up here that most of the accommodations are suites, which means more work for the maid in each one. Also, Gene Knight told me that the maid in question was working just beyond this suite, so the second caller didn't pass her on his way here. Am I clear so far?"

When no one spoke, Tibbs continued. "I clocked the average time it takes to make up a suite; it's twenty-two minutes. To walk from the elevators to this door takes about nineteen seconds; I tried it several times. That makes the odds about sixty-five to one that the maid doing the rooms would have been at work inside the next suite and not in the corridor to see the second visitor. She could have come out to get some supplies, but when I watched her, she never did that. An experienced hotel maid doesn't make unnecessary motions.

"Which brings us to the maid who was vacuuming. I

couldn't talk to her because of the language barrier, but I was able to study her work. She was using an industrial-type upright that is solidly built and makes a certain amount of noise. Each time she does the hallway, she begins at the elevators, where the most traffic is, and works down the hallway to the end. She covers about six and a half feet per minute once she is past the elevators.

"Gene Knight showed me where she was when he came up with 'Smith'. In approximately four and a half minutes she would have worked her way past this suite, so she would have been farther down the hallway, *with her back to the area between the elevators and the door.*

"Now three small, but important points. The vacuum cleaner makes enough noise to cover anyone coming up the hallway, or even a subdued knock on a door. While we're on the subject of noise, I asked if the rooms on this floor have any additional soundproofing and was told that they do. That and the noise of the cleaner would cover the sound of a shot from a small-caliber weapon with the door closed.

"The second point is the way a vacuum cleaner is used. The person working with one invariably keeps his or her attention on the carpet being cleaned, unless he stops to rest. Everyone using a vacuum cleaner does that, watching what he or she is doing, checking that the cleaner is picking up any tiny scraps or other debris, and avoiding hitting furniture or the baseboards.

"The third point is the testimony of the maids. I read the transcript very carefully, in translation. They were each asked, 'Did you see anyone come in or out of suite twenty-two eighteen between two-thirty and three o'clock?' Both answered no. They were then asked if they had left work for any reason. Both again answered no. They were then asked if they were sure, and they both answered yes. They were *not* asked, '*Could* anyone have gone in or out of suite

167

twenty-two eighteen while you were there?' "

Virgil stopped and waited. After several seconds he went on. "Now I believe you can see what happened. Smith was escorted to the door of twenty-two eighteen and was admitted. Knight waited outside until he was called away. Shortly after that the American agent came to the door, unobserved by either of the maids, and knocked. Smith let him in and then shot him, with Miriam's gun. Even if Smith didn't know who the American was, it didn't matter: he'd been caught in the suite with Miriam lying unconscious on the floor. A man like him wouldn't hesitate a moment. He probably took a few seconds to put the gun in Miriam's hand and then just left. Who would question seeing a man walk peacefully out of a hotel room? The lobby is huge and usually well filled with all kinds of people. He could get out without going anywhere near the desk, and probably did."

It was very quiet for almost half a minute, then Lee gently nodded his head.

Millbrae stood up. "It fits," he said. "You're all right, mate. I'll get out a report."

As soon as Millbrae had gone, Lee got to his feet. "Tonight, Virgil," he said, "you and the lady are going to have dinner with me. No arguments. I have a place in mind. Pick you up about seven."

"We accept with pleasure," Miriam said, "but I can't leave the hotel."

"I'd forgotten that," Lee admitted. "All right, we'll eat upstairs, or in the Chinese restaurant, whichever you prefer."

When the dinner was over, Virgil prowled the city for almost three hours, turning off into many of the byways and some dark alleys, but there was no sign of anyone taking an interest in what he was doing. He returned to the hotel well after midnight, let himself quietly into the suite, and went to bed.

He was very tired, so much so that at first he was not even aware when Miriam quietly slid into the bed beside him. When he at last sensed her presence, he turned on his side toward her.

"Virgil," she said very softly. "Forgive me, but I'm frightened. I just can't stand being alone anymore."

"I understand," he said. He wanted to reach out and comfort her, but sensing that she had more to say, he waited.

"I did love my husband so very much." He could barely hear her, she spoke so softly. "I still can't accept the fact that I'll never see him again. Not on this earth, anyway. And I miss my children."

He understood then, completely.

She moved her head until it was a few inches from his—facing him in the dark. "Virgil, can I stay here a little while, just to be with you? I know it isn't fair—"

He laid a finger across her lips. "Of course," he said. "Would you like me to hold you?"

"Please, if it isn't asking too much. You see, I just can't . . ."

"I don't want you to," he answered. He gathered her gently to him and stroked her hair with his right hand, as he had once comforted a dog left in the road by a hit-and-run driver. The dog had rewarded him with a look of burning gratitude. Compassion, he knew, crossed all barriers and knew no limitations.

"Virgil, tell me that it's going to be all right."

"It's going to be all right," he repeated. "You've done nothing wrong. Everyone knows that now."

"Thanks to you."

"It would have come out anyway. The people here know what they're doing."

She had nothing to say after that. She remained for a long time resting quietly beside the man who had come to her rescue. She could not sleep, because in her mind images were forming and colliding with one another: the man she had married, the country she had made her new home, the children she had borne—and the realization that so much of it all was gone forever. She seemed to hear her husband's voice again, and she longed for him across the months they had been forever separated.

Then like an asteroid tumbling through space she saw the image of the fine and decent man who lay beside her and who had accepted her presence on her terms, difficult as it must be for him. She wondered if she was being grossly unfair to him, if she was thinking too much about the past. She determined to resolve that question in her mind when she would be wide awake and in the full possession of her faculties.

For a moment she was tempted to throw everything else aside and give herself to him, because he was a very special person in her life, and because she wanted to. Then she saw that he was asleep. Once again she was aware of the great control he had over himself, and the price he had paid to acquire it. Very carefully she slipped away from him, got to her feet, and feeling very much unlike herself, retreated to her own bedroom.

Chapter Twenty

When she woke in the morning, the sun was already streaming in through the windows of her bedroom. She got up, slipped on a dressing gown, and opened the door to the large sitting room of the suite.

Virgil was standing in the middle of the floor, clad only in a pair of shapeless white cotton pants. There was a fine perspiration covering the top half of his body except the area covered by the dressings, where he had been shot. He remained still, his arms held vertically in front of his body, his fists tightly clenched. Then he broke into startling motion. With the muscles of his torso tense under his dark skin, he spun his body, snapped out lightninglike kicks right and left, and punched with concentrated speed and power toward two or three imaginary opponents.

She was almost frightened by the startling change; the quiet and restrained man she thought she knew was suddenly an awesome lethal weapon. The unleashed but disciplined power made her hold her breath until Virgil drew his feet together and resumed his starting pose. He held it for a moment, then relaxed. When he turned to pick up a towel, he saw her for the first time. "What was that?" she asked.

Virgil smiled at her. "It was a kata, a formal karate exercise where every movement is supposed to be done exactly right in a certain order. That was *teki shodan,* a fairly simple one. I have to go easy, because my side is still very tender."

She looked at the firm muscular pattern of his body and shook her head. "Go take a shower," she said. "Then I have something for you."

It took Tibbs ten minutes to shave and shower to his satisfaction. He was just starting to dress when Miriam tapped on the door. When Virgil opened it, she came in and laid a tissue-wrapped package on the bed. "I've seen so many other handsome men wearing these Singapore safari suits, I got one for you. Put it on; I'd like to see how you look in it."

"I'll see if it fits," Tibbs said with some reluctance.

"I'm sure it does: I took the hotel tailor one of your other suits to measure."

Obediently Virgil slipped into a lightweight pair of cream-colored trousers. As he adjusted them around his hips, they fitted perfectly.

"Now an undershirt and the bush jacket," Miriam said, taking a full interest in the proceedings. Tibbs complied and then pulled the short-sleeve jacket down until it was properly set on his shoulders. "I like it!" she said.

Virgil walked a few steps and was surprised at the comfort of the unfamiliar suit. "Thank you," he said.

"Is that the best you can do?"

He took her into his arms and kissed her with gentle, deep feeling. "That's better," she said. "Now let's go down to breakfast."

They were three-quarters of the way through the meal when the hostess came to tell Virgil that he was wanted on the telephone. When he picked up the instrument, a feminine voice greeted him. "Mr. Tibbs, Deputy Commissioner Sim's compliments and could you be here to see him at nine?"

There was only one possible answer to that; he gave it and then returned to his unfinished meal. "I'm wanted at the Head Shed," he said. "I'm sorry but I've got to leave you again."

"When will you be back?"

"I don't know."

"So be it," Miriam accepted. "But I so wish I could just walk up and down on Orchard Road, look into some shops, and breathe some real, un-conditioned air."

"I know," Virgil said. "I don't think it will be for too much longer. Just remember how much better it is than—"

"Don't finish," Miriam said quickly. "I was wrong to complain."

Tibbs signed the check, then he went outside to be greeted by the rising heat of the day. He glanced at his watch and took a cab to the main police building. It was on the side of a small hill with several entrances down its long length. He had the cab drop him at the second one and went inside. "Virgil Tibbs to see Deputy Commissioner Sim, by appointment," he told the officer behind the reception desk.

Four minutes later he was shown into Sim's office. The deputy commissioner rose to greet him with a polite and affable smile. "Good morning, Mr. Tibbs," he said and offered his hand. Even if he was a product of Chinese culture, he understood Western manners perfectly.

"Could I ask you to drop the mister?" Tibbs asked.

"Yes, of course. And what a nice suit that is. I have several myself. Please sit down. How about some iced tea?"

That was a concession; iced tea was not usually offered at a police facility.

"Thank you," Tibbs said.

Sim used the phone briefly and then turned to his visitor. "Since your meeting with Lee and the others in the hotel suite yesterday, you've kept us quite busy," he began. "Lee reported your conversation to Superintendent Subramaniam. In turn he got hold of Superintendent Osman Mohamed, whom I believe you know, and told him that the case against Madam Motamboru wouldn't wash anymore. Osman called me. I then talked with Lee and got the story firsthand. Can you guess what happened next?"

"You called Judge Goh," Tibbs suggested.

"I must arrange to have you give a lecture at our Academy, Virgil. That's exactly what I did. When I had talked with him, I sent a hand-delivered letter to Ambassador Thatcher. In it I told him that new evidence, developed by yourself, had resulted in the decision to drop the charges against Madam Motamboru."

"That's very good news, sir."

Sim was in a mood to be generous. "I have to say, Virgil, that I admire the way you've discharged your mission here. If we had some doubts, they were based only on the odds against you."

Sim stopped when there was a tap on the door and the refreshments were brought in. The deputy commissioner had hot tea. Virgil's iced tea was on a par with most police station coffee, but he accepted it with every show of gratitude.

When they were again alone, Sim relaxed a little behind his desk. "This is very much off the record," he said, "but ours is an unusual society here and not everyone who comes by knows how to cope with it. We're happy to welcome you as a friend."

"That's a great honor, sir," Tibbs said.

"Thank you. Now, I have a request to make. Your assignment here, as far as your government is concerned, is completed with distinction. We are now convinced of Madam's innocence, but unfortunately that doesn't give us any ammunition to shoot down outside criticism."

Virgil drank some iced tea and waited.

174

"Lee tells me you're fully aware of the diplomatic and propaganda aspects of the Motamboru case. Officially, she's free to leave whenever she wishes. But we would be grateful if both of you would agree to maintain the status quo until we have arrested the man who calls himself John Smith. It should only be a day or two, at the most."

"What you are saying, sir, is that you want to bust him for the homicide in Mrs. Motamboru's suite. When you have him in custody on that charge, then, as we would say, the heat will be off."

For the first time Sim paid some attention to his tea. "I must learn to appreciate iced tea," he said, "then I won't have to worry about it getting cold all the time. Now, another matter. In order not to waste the talents of a person of your ability—"

"Please," Virgil interrupted.

"All right, then—your friend Lee has asked if you would be willing to spend a little time with him on the Tan killings. To be his pro tem partner. You had a partner at home?"

"Yes, a very good one. Bob Nakamura."

"Nakamura—a Japanese?"

"No, sir. Bob is as American as I am."

Sim drank tea. "My apologies," he said.

Tibbs changed the subject. "I have one reservation, sir. The other members of the department might not appreciate—"

"I took care of that," Sim said. "Technically I'm inviting you to observe our methods, as my guest."

"When may I begin?"

"Whenever you'd like. My secretary has a copy of the Tan case file for you, in case you wish to read it. Please tell Madam that we much regret having to ask her to stay in the hotel, but I'm sure she understands."

Tibbs stood up. "Thank you, sir," he said.

*   *   *

175

As soon as he was back at the hotel, Tibbs went to the medical suite to have his dressings changed. Dr. Ling was as coolly efficient as before, taking his temperature and blood pressure before she removed the old dressings. She examined the wound and spread a healing gel over the reddened area. The fresh dressing that she applied was still too large for comfort, but Tibbs did not argue about it. He sensed that it would do no good.

As soon as he was back in the suite, he sat down and began going over the case file on the Tan killings. Miriam was careful to leave him undisturbed. When it was past one o'clock he broke his concentration long enough to take her down to the coffee shop, where he had his usual lunch of a sandwich and a milkshake. As soon as he was finished he excused himself and went back up to the suite to continue his work. He was still at it when the phone rang at a little after four.

It was Lee calling. "When I was in Pasadena, you took me out with you on a case," he said. "Now I can return the favor. I understand you have the file."

"I'm just going over it for the fifth time," Virgil answered.

"Have you dug anything out yet?"

"I have a couple of ideas. When would you like to start?"

"How about in the morning? I'll pick you up at nine."

"See you then."

As soon as Tibbs put the phone down, there was a tap on the door. Knowing that hotel security would be covering all visitors, he opened the door and discovered that Jack Myers was outside. "Come in," he invited.

Myers did so and then looked around. "Is the lady here?" he asked.

"No, she left after lunch. I don't know where she went."

"Okay." Myers sat down and leaned forward, indicating that he wanted to talk business while he had the opportunity. "I know about your interview with Arthur Sim this morning," he began. "He called and put me in the picture. You really pulled it off, Virgil. You have my thanks now; you'll get some official ones later."

"I'm glad it worked out," Tibbs said.

"I also know you've been invited to join the Tan investigation. Virgil, that's a hell of an honor. No matter who you are at home, you're an outsider here. They've made you a member of the lodge. I hope you understand what that means."

"I think I do."

"Just remember how much face means over here. They're giving you a lot of theirs. I brought you some things. You need an international driver's license; here it is. Can you make out driving on the left?"

"I'll try."

"Secondly, I've got a car for you. It has diplomatic plates, so it's exempt from the center city restrictions."

"I'm not sure I need it," Tibbs said.

"Take it, and don't ask too many questions."

"Whatever you say."

"The doorman has the keys. Whenever you come back here, he'll park it for you. How are you fixed for funds?"

"I've actually spent very little. I've been signing tabs."

"Here's a thousand Singapore dollars. If you eat with the brass, large or small, pick up the check. It's proper courtesy here. I know you'd like to go home, but there are good reasons why you're being asked to stay."

"Anything else?" Tibbs asked.

"Just let me know how things are going. Don't ask for receipts; you won't need them. Let it appear that you're the host."

"I'll do that," Tibbs said.

"Good. I'll keep in touch."

He had only been gone a few minutes when Miriam returned. "We are having dinner in the suite this evening," she announced.

"Honestly," Virgil told her, "I'd rather not."

"Would it make any difference if I told you that I'm going to cook it?"

Virgil looked at her. "How did you manage that?" he asked.

Miriam gave him a slightly wicked smile. "The master chef is French, and I have some good recipes. It's been a little boring, not being able to go out, so we became friends."

"In his language, I assume."

"Yes, of course. Anyhow, I've arranged to cook for you whenever you'd like."

"Miriam, you're wonderful." He meant it very sincerely.

"Wait until you've tried your dinner."

"I don't have to. I know what you can do. You gave me the best food I've ever had in my life."

The dinner, which featured Swedish fruit soup, rack of lamb with garden vegetables, and cherries jubilee, was a heavenly delight. Virgil had never wanted to become a gourmet; it didn't go with a policeman's job. But Miriam's cooking could create a palate in any man. Despite the surroundings of the suite, where so much had happened, the dinner was an occasion. The candles on the table served a dual purpose: they created a gentle, intimate light for dining and beyond it allowed an enveloping darkness, one that effectively obliterated all the stresses and strains of the unseen world left hidden in the shadows.

When it was over, Virgil stood up and stretched out his arms to flex the muscles that had been inactive too long. Miriam watched and then spoke very calmly. "Will you answer some questions for me?" she asked.

Virgil looked at her. "Of course—if I can."

178

"About how many policemen are there in Singapore?"

He saw at once the point she was about to make, but he kept that knowledge to himself. "More than six thousand," he answered.

"Are they good?"

"Very good. In a city like this they would have to be— and they are."

He walked toward her until they were close enough to touch, but he left his arms at his sides. "Let's sit together for a moment," he proposed.

Obediently Miriam sat down on one of the large sofas in the suite. Virgil took his place beside her.

"I'm going to level with you," he began, "and that's another American expression you can add to your repertoire. I've never been a field agent; I don't expect that I will ever become one. Certainly not in this part of the world." There was no need for him to explain further. "But I know what kind of people they are and how they operate. Over the years in Pasadena we had constant dealings with the Secret Service and other agencies. I've had many confidential briefings, so I know a little about it. I think you do too."

"That's true," Miriam acknowledged.

"You know, then, something of the KGB and how it operates."

"Much more than I like."

Virgil reached out and took her hand. It lay very soft and gentle in his own. "Miriam, that organization isn't the best in the world, but it's one of the most ruthless. It won't condone failure. Only under impossible circumstances will it accept defeat. 'John Smith' is KGB. It's too late for him to prevent your husband's report from reaching Washington without creating an incident that would backfire all over the world. That price would be too high."

"I understand all that," Miriam said.

"So there's only one way that 'Smith' can salvage some

of his mission: by taking you out. He can't go home until he does. There's no possible way a Fifth Directorate killer like himself could explain failure to eliminate one woman who, in this environment, stands out in a crowd. I didn't want to spell it out like this, but you'd better know the truth."

Miriam turned her body until she could put her hands on his shoulders. "I'm going to be just as direct," she said. "In Pasadena you carried a gun, because it was part of your job. You don't have one here."

"I know that, Miriam, and I feel naked without my weapon. Especially because 'Smith' wants you. That's why Arthur Sim asked you not to leave the hotel. I'm sure he's got some of his best people watching over you around the clock."

"You mean the suite is bugged?"

"No, he wouldn't do that. But in this hotel, where so many Americans and Europeans stay, 'Smith' wouldn't be conspicuous. So it comes down to this: if he isn't taken out, one way or another, he'll pursue you wherever you go until he gets you. Otherwise he's a dead man: his own service would dump him, and they have one technique for that. To him I'm your bodyguard, the main obstacle between him and you. So I can draw him out."

Miriam sat very still until the air in the room seemed motionless. "Virgil," she said. "You're very, very good—I know that. But he's an armed professional killer. I don't want you to go up against him, not alone. Especially when he can choose the time and place." Tears welled up in her eyes. "Don't you see what I mean?" she asked.

He drew her closer to him. "Of course I do, Miriam, but it isn't quite that bad. Because perhaps I can pick the time and place. And I may not be quite as foolhardy as you think. When I meet him, he may find that he has his hands fuller than he expected."

Chapter Twenty-One

Less than a minute later the phone rang. Tibbs answered to find Lee on the line. "I'm in the lobby," the Singapore detective said. "May I come up?"

Three minutes later Lee was ushered in by a member of the security staff. His identity was well known, but the hotel was following its own rigid rules.

Miriam was at once the perfect hostess. "Superintendent Lee, we're delighted to see you," she said. "I'll send for coffee and dessert."

"Don't," Lee retorted. "I may not be as welcome as you think."

"What's happened?" Tibbs asked.

Lee chose to ignore the question; instead he asked one of his own. "How much confidence do you have in our department?" He looked from one to the other, waiting for his answer.

Miriam spoke first. "Obviously you want us to do something—something that involves a risk."

"That's right," Lee admitted.

It was Tibbs's turn. "Roger, are you asking Miriam to bait a trap?"

"Yes," Lee said. He leaned forward a little and put his hands on his knees. "I've just come from a meeting with

Arthur Sim, Pandian Subramaniam, and the top people of our Special Enforcement Team. Virgil, you haven't seen any of them yet, but take my word for it, they're good."

"I do," Tibbs said.

"Virgil, I don't have to tell you that the best source of information in police work is informants, or snitches as you call them. We have a good network here in Singapore."

"I would assume that."

"Good. The way this town is laid out, 'Smith,' as he calls himself, could lie low for some time, despite that fact that most of our population is Oriental. Digging him out would be a very hard job. Remember, he's a pro in a very tough service."

Tibbs drew breath to speak, but Lee held up a hand to stop him. "Yesterday a man cleared immigration and left Singapore using a passport we recognized as belonging to 'Smith,' never mind how. But it was a blind. 'Smith,' we think, is still here."

"If I understand you," Miriam interjected, "This man wanted you to recognize 'Smith's' passport he was using. Didn't he risk arrest at the airport?"

"On what charge?" Lee responded. "We don't have anything that will stick; no witness to prove that 'Smith' killed a man in this room. So we let him go; we had to. Only it wasn't 'Smith,' if a reliable informant is right."

"So now you want to draw 'Smith' out," Tibbs said. "He's got to move fast, because Miriam has been sprung, and she could leave tomorrow if she chooses."

Lee offered a grim smile. "We managed to spread that word, not too openly, around town."

"What do you want us to do?" Miriam asked.

Lee was very careful how he laid it out. "We've been doing some plotting of our own. First, we've shown all the signs of believing that 'Smith' has left Singapore and is out of our hair. We had a travel agent call several airlines to inquire about flights to Switzerland for Madam Motamboru."

"For heaven's sake, call me Miriam."

"Gladly," Lee answered. "Roger here. We've made some other waves that a pro like 'Smith' will be almost sure to pick up."

"If he doesn't smell a rat," Tibbs noted.

"We were pretty careful to see that he doesn't. As you might say, Virgil, we weren't born yesterday."

"Question," Tibbs interrupted. "Is Jack Myers in on this?"

"Yes."

"Is that why he suddenly provided me with a car I didn't ask for?"

"You've got it."

Lee waited a moment while his friend put the pieces together. It didn't take long. "This evening you want me to take Miriam out in the car, presumably to celebrate the fact that her troubles are over. We'll be seen leaving the hotel. But any place I might take her will be public, making it very difficult for your swat team to cover her."

"Go on."

"He might take a shot at her in the car, but it would be risky."

"The car has bulletproof glass."

"And easily recognized diplomatic plates."

"Yes."

"Since it's well after dinner, we won't be going to a restaurant. Possibly for a drink, but there are several very good bars here in the hotel."

"On the other hand," Lee continued for him, "Miriam has been shut up here for some time. She might enjoy just getting out for a while: a joy ride, I think you call it."

"What's our route?" Tibbs asked.

"Talk to the doorman outside the hotel. Ask him to direct you to the road up Mount Faber, to see the lights of the city. Your route is down Orchard Road, past the new Raffles Center, and to the harbor area to see the Singapore lion. Then around the city, as you like. Finally up Mount Faber to arrive there at or about eleven-forty. Stay awhile and admire the view."

"Are we to get out of the car?"

"Give us five minutes first after your arrival. And, Virgil, I know your skills, but leave this one to us. You're still recuperating, and we'll be well prepared."

"What are the chances that he'll try for us there?"

"Good enough that we're gambling on it. When you see the location, you'll know why. It's the only place in Singapore that's sufficiently isolated and that you'd be likely to go."

"Then a lot of others could be there also."

"Not tonight, but leave that to us."

Tibbs became very businesslike. "Miriam, do you want to risk this? You know it's dangerous."

"If you had been in Bakara with me," Miriam answered, "you wouldn't ask that. I've faced much worse, many times."

Tibbs turned to Lee. "How long will it take to climb the hill?"

"Two or three minutes; it's negligible. We'll be in position well before you get there, so if you're a little early, don't worry." He turned to Miriam. "You won't see us, but be assured we'll have you both covered. If it comes to that, there are two world-class sharpshooters on the team."

"One more question," Tibbs interjected. "If our man does show up, is he likely to have any help with him?"

"I can't answer that," Lee said.

Since Singapore is never cold, Virgil chose a pair of lightweight trousers and a knit sports shirt to go out. He had more than simple comfort in mind as he picked what he would wear; he was interested too in maximum body freedom. With Miriam coming with him, he wanted every possible advantage he could get. He declined Lee's suggestion that he borrow a Second Chance vest and also the offer of a gun. He had his reasons for both decisions; an unfamiliar weapon was not part of his personal plan.

With his wallet in his pocket and little else, he rode down with Miriam at his side, crossed the lobby, and spoke to the doorman. "I understand that a car as been left here for me."

"Yes, Mr. Tibbs. Shall I have it brought around for you?"

"Please. And can you direct me to Mount Faber." He made it a statement, not a question.

"Very easily; I'll draw you a map. Have you been there yet?"

"No," Tibbs said.

"It's not much more than a low hill," the doorman explained. "It does give you a fair view of the city. There is a temple up there and some Buddhist statuary, if that interests you." He stepped to his desk and sketched a simple map. Not long after he finished, a sleek yellow sports car rolled up and stopped.

"Here is your car, sir," the doorman added. "And a map."

"Thank you." Tibbs got into the trim, low-slung car as the doorman assisted Miriam into the other side. Fortunately the traffic was light on Orchard Road. Driving on the left was very awkward for Virgil, but he found he could manage. He turned right toward the harbor and started to roll down a window until he remembered.

Shortly after that two cars trying to enter the Mount Faber road at the same time collided and were locked together. Each driver adamantly blamed the other until the police arrived. Meanwhile several other cars that wanted to go up the Mount Faber road had to turn away. The accident took some time to clear; it was past eleven when the roadway was once again open.

After driving about for some time, Virgil found the Mount Faber entrance road and started up the gentle grade that led to the top. The time was exactly eleven thirty-eight.

When he arrived there he discovered a level parking area that was virtually deserted. At the edge, the lights of Singapore were visible through the trees that covered the upper part of the low hill.

For a few minutes he sat quietly with Miriam, almost feeling the tension in her body and admiring the appearance of external calmness that she was able to maintain. He looked carefully, but there was no evidence that they were not entirely alone on the low hilltop.

After carefully calculating the odds, he turned to Miriam and said, "Would you like to see the temple?"

"Yes," she answered.

He got out of the car and helped her to her feet. Then he turned and looked at the temple. He saw what appeared to be a long open room with a far altar and beyond it a large statue of the Buddha. The altar was covered with a variety of objects, including two tall flower vases that were filled with fresh blooms. A faint hint of incense touched the air. Obviously those who came were invited to enter.

He took Miriam's arm as they walked inside and halfway up the room. Then he stopped, feeling the atmosphere of peace that surrounded him. Mixed with it was his awareness of the peculiar magic of Oriental art, in some cases wonderfully simple, in others so intricate as to be unbelievable. Much thoughtful care had gone into the design of the temple that surrounded them, enough to make him wish that he could sit quietly and meditate while the world outside became equally peaceful. But that he would not live to see. Out of respect for a great religion, and those whose dedicated labor had created the temple that was easing his spirit at that moment, he put his hands together and bowed his head slightly for a moment, offering his thanks. Then he took Miriam outside to meet whatever awaited them there. As he did so, adrenaline flooded his body, and he was alert for the slightest sound or movement.

For a moment he sharply regretted having allowed Miriam, a civilian, to be with him, but that decision could not be changed. He was acutely aware that a single shot from ambush, even in the thin moonlight, could drop her where she stood. He was counting completely on the unseen Special Enforcement Team to eliminate that possibility.

The parking lot was visibly empty. He stopped and took a deep breath; he was letting it out of his lungs when he caught the faintest suggestion of a sound behind him.

In a split second he bent at the waist, taking the top half of his body out of a possible target area. He saw feet almost directly behind him; the man had been amazingly silent. He threw his body down, folding his left knee as his palms hit the surface of the ground. With all his strength he kicked backward with his right foot at a thirty-degree upward angle. The back snap-kick landed solidly close to the groin, momentarily throwing the man behind him off balance. That gave Tibbs a precious second to whirl to his feet and face him. The man was not too clear in the moonlight, but he was just over six feet with powerfully shaped shoulders and a full head of blond hair.

Because the man was far enough away to allow him time to speak, Virgil drew a quick full breath and said, "Mr. Smith, I believe."

His opponent was unruffled. In a flat voice, totally devoid of accent or emotion, he said, "You are in the way."

They remained still, each using every passing moment to appraise the other. Then the blond man spoke again. "You need not try your karate. The last man I killed was a karate master."

Virgil showed no reaction. He stood perfectly still and waited.

The blond man, with almost agonizing slowness, reached

out his arm; when he brought it back a long slim knife blade was protruding from his hand. Still Tibbs made no move, standing like a dark statue in the moonlight.

"Whenever you're ready," the man said.

"Make your move," Virgil replied.

Even in the darkness he could see the man lift the knife slightly, not in the edge-up street-fighting position, but half crosswise as only an expert would do. Against that, Virgil maintained rigid control, keeping his lungs full of air and only exhaling as much as was absolutely necessary.

In a flash of lightning speed the rock-hard blond man was upon him. It was incredibly fast: Tibbs had not believed a human could move with such concerted, violent energy. Despite his careful preparation, he was almost overwhelmed. With his weight on his left foot, he snapped his body sideways and thrust his hands toward the blond man's right wrist. His fingers found their target, not in a hard grip, but with his thumbs on one side, his first two fingers on the other.

The instant he had that much, he spun his body in a right snap turn, raising his arms just high enough to clear his head. In a fraction of a second he had his opponent's arm doubled at the elbow, his wrist locked in the deadly grip of *Kote-Gaeshi*. Then with concerted force he snapped both of his arms down, forcing his opponent's wrist to twist outside and away from his body. The blond man dropped instantly to relieve the pressure, but he could not hold the knife. Ignoring the intense pain, he cocked his right leg to smash it into Tibbs's groin.

Virgil dropped with him, adding iron-hard pressure until his opponent's wrist snapped out of joint. With that movement he completed *Ushiro Hiji-Tori*, one of the deadliest and most effective techinques of aikido.

The blond man was on his feet like a tiger, but his right hand was helpless. Virgil saw that he held a second knife in his left hand, its blade visible in the moonlight. He lifted his weight onto the balls of his feet, ready to move with the greatest speed of which he was capable. He had gained a momentary advantage; but he was facing an opponent with almost inhuman training and skill.

He forced himself to take advantage of the great principle of aikido: to remain still and let the opponent attack. His long years of karate training almost violently urged him to attack, but he knew that if he tried that, he would be doomed. The blond man was too good. So he held his balance, controlled his breathing, and kept his eyes intently on his opponent's feet.

He saw the left Achilles tendon tighten and was warned. With reflexes that he had honed for years in the *dojo* he waited for the exact instant, knowing that his opponent might kick, butt, or snap the knife into his abdomen—if he could. This time he lunged forward himself to throw off his opponent's timing. It was a dangerous gamble; the blond man had anticipated it and was ready. At the last fraction of a second Tibbs spun to his right and caught the man's left wrist in *Katate-tori Ryote-mochi Nikyo.* It was a complex move, but he had done it countless times in practice. The blond man went down, but he drew up his legs to jump to his feet in less than a second. At the moment that the soles of his feet hit the pavement, Tibbs delivered a powerful, expertly controlled front snap-kick into his opponent's groin.

The cold ruthlessness that had taken possession of him let him deliver the merciless blow. He knew the awful agony that had to be in his opponent's body, but the man stood poised on the balls of his feet, waiting for the next move. It was by no means over.

"Freeze!"

The amplified voice rang out with sharp authority as sudden beams of stabbing bright light almost simultaneously cut across the parking area from several directions. The forms of black-clad men were all around them, closing in. Two of them stayed where they were, down on one knee, holding rifles with rigid accuracy.

Tibbs did not look at them: he kept his attention fixed on his deadly opponent as the man snapped back his left arm to throw the knife at the motionless figure of Miriam. With a totally concentrated burst of energy Virgil flung himself forward and high in the arm. He jerked up his knees and delivered a smashing drop-kick at his opponent's upper body. The knife arced in the air and dropped harmlessly onto the pavement as the blond man took the full force of the blow. For a moment he staggered back; in that time Tibbs landed on his feet, swept his opponent's legs from under him, and with ice-cold fury delivered a paralyzing heel ram into his abdomen. The wind went out of the man's body and he lay still.

Virgil looked up then to see that Miriam was surrounded by six men with deadly looking weapons. At least eight more were around him and the now-motionless agent on the ground. One of them, whom he did not recognize, spoke to Virgil. "Thank you, Mr. Tibbs. You were covered, but we wanted him alive if possible."

Although he was breathing hard, Virgil answered as calmly as he was able. "Of course. Otherwise an innocent tourist came to see the view and was gunned down without provocation by the police."

"Glad you're a member of the lodge. Inspector Fong here."

An efficient sergeant took over the man who called himself John Smith. "Bring over the ambulance," he directed. "I don't think he can walk."

Lee materialized from somewhere and walked over to Tibbs. "How are you?" he asked.

"Fine, thanks," Virgil answered.

"We could have nailed him several times, but you had

things under control. That last drop-kick was a beaut."

"I don't know how many times I practiced that until I learned it," Tibbs said. "Tonight it paid off."

Lee looked at him, and his attitude abruptly changed. "Your side, it's bloody!"

"I know, I probably ripped out some stitches." He suddenly felt a little weak, until he was aware that Miriam was beside him. An ambulance drew up.

"We had it standing by, with a doctor," Lee said. "Get in and lie down: he'll look after you."

"Thanks, but—"

"Do it!" Miriam said. He took one look at her determined face and climbed into the back of the vehicle. The thing was settled now; there was more than enough help on hand, so he resigned himself while the deft fingers of a nurse took off his shirt. The doctor, who was a Muslim, ordered him to lie down and then set to work. Miriam sat on the spare seat, twisting and untwisting her fingers in tense anxiety as she watched the surface blood being swabbed away. She wished desperately that she could do it for him, but she knew that the doctor's hands were more skilled than her own.

Tibbs's body was shaking slightly, a reaction against the intense concentration to which it had been subjected. He wanted to go and soak in a steaming tub of hot water, but that was out of the question. He lay still until he had been taped up, then he got very stiffly to his feet.

Lee was waiting for him just outside. "How did you get the drop on him?" he asked. "You know his reputation."

"He expected me to try karate," Virgil answered. "He said so. He wasn't expecting aikido. That was my edge. I was counting on it."

"I'll have you and Miriam taken back in one of our cars. Yours will be dropped off with the doorman. Statements can wait until morning."

"Thanks," Tibbs said. He ceased to care too much after

191

that. He was aware that Miriam sat close to him, holding his right hand in both of hers, and it was pleasant. He was able at last to relax, mentally and physically. Lee was in the front seat with the driver. "Is that stuff hard to learn?" he asked without warning.

Tibbs was not in the mood for anything but the cold truth. "It takes years," he answered.

"I thought so."

The car turned onto Orchard Road, the driver maintaining an easy smooth pace.

Presently he turned into the entrance driveway of the Crossroads and eased to a stop before the door. Lee got out and assisted Miriam, who was still visibly shaken. "Rather an interesting evening," he commented.

"I found it so," Miriam answered, and turned to Virgil, who was getting to his own feet a little more slowly than usual.

Tibbs looked at his friend. "Now can I go home?" he asked.

"Yes," Lee answered, "of course. After a few formalities. And as soon as the Tan case is over."

Chapter Twenty-Two

When Tibbs awoke in the morning after a painful and restless night, the message light on his phone was blinking. He picked up the instrument and dialed the hotel operator.

"Mr. Tibbs, you have a message from Superintendent Lee," the girl reported. "It says, 'In view of our carousing last night, I suggest we cancel our appointment this morning. I'll call you later.' The message is signed 'Roger.' "

"Thank you," Tibbs said, and sank back in bed with a deep sense of gratitude. The way he was, the less he had to do the better. His side throbbed with pain and not a muscle in his body felt comfortable. He longed for a hot shower, knowing that it was not possible and probably wouldn't be for some time. Then he realized he was feeling sorry for himself. That he would not tolerate; slowly and carefully he got to his feet and began to put on his clothes. He was just completing that uncomfortable process when the suite doorbell rang.

Although he had not yet shaved, he went to see who it was. Miriam, who was up, dressed, and looking her best, opened the door to admit Tom Millbrae. "I've just learned that Virgil got banged up last night," he said. "I came to see how he is."

"I ripped out some stitches," Tibbs answered. "But in a good cause."

"So I heard. You must be a helluva fighter, mate; the word is you took out a top man from the opposition bare-handed."

"There were more guys there than you could count," Tibbs said. "The police had their Special Enforcement Team up there."

"They're all stout lads, I know, but you had your man down and out, Lee told me. Have you had breakfast yet?"

"I haven't even combed my hair."

"Eat first, then you have an appointment in medical. After that I've booked you for a massage in the health club, on the house."

"I don't feel like a massage," Tibbs said.

"You don't know our massage people. They'll take the kinks out and give you a hot sponge bath at the same time. No arguments. Tucker first, then you get the works."

Miriam put down the phone. "I've just ordered breakfast," she said. "Hot cakes, eggs, sausage, toast, and coffee. Please join us."

"I can't," Millbrae answered. "Also I've had mine. But see that man of yours gets a good feed. Nothing like it to build back the strength." With that he let himself out.

By the time the meal arrived, Tibbs had shaved and otherwise made himself presentable. He sat down with Miriam and ate with much more relish than he had expected. His side still pounded out its steady-beat agony while he did his best to ignore it.

At the medical department he at last met Dr. Singh. Unlike many Sikhs, he was not a tall man, but his ability was clear. He checked Tibbs over with brisk thoroughness, then offered a suggestion: "A day or two in hospital, while your side knits again, might be a good idea."

"I can't," Tibbs answered. "I've got work I must do."

"Nothing strenuous, I trust."

"I'm planning to go to the library."

"Why the library, may I ask?"

"Because there's more information there than anywhere else. Ouch!"

"Sorry, sir, but I now have to work on the damaged area. This is a local anesthetic; it will take hold very quickly. You won't feel the rest of the shots at all."

An hour and a half later, his side still numb, Tibbs was at the library, delving into the customs and practices of the northern China district from which Madam Wee had come. Once again he had his long legal pad on which he was making careful and detailed notes. With the aid of an efficient assistant he also dug out certain facts about the governmental policies in that area. He had seen a television documentary on the subject, but he wanted more specific data and, if possible, from entirely reliable sources.

Because of the huge breakfast he had eaten, he skipped lunch and worked through. When he had finished, he called the Leong Shipyards and asked for an appointment with the managing director. That proved a little difficult; the man's secretary informed Tibbs that at least a week would be required to set up an open time and why, please, did he want to see Mr. Khan?

Without revealing too much, Tibbs managed to wrangle a fifteen-minute slot at four-fifteen. Satisfied, he went back to the hotel to lie down until it was time for him to keep the appointment. The local had worn off, and his side hurt like hell.

He took a cab to the shipyard and was deposited before the executive offices. In the lobby he went through the usual reception formalities before he was shown up to the managing director's suite. There he was invited to sit down and offered coffee for what he hoped would be a short wait. The secretary who had been difficult on the phone was all courtesy and consideration.

He had not half finished his coffee when he was shown

into a huge corner office that overlooked the shipyard proper. It was heavily soundproofed; the windows were coated with a blue tint that cut much of the heat of the sun. Khan himself was in his sixties, dark-skinned, well-groomed, and dressed in a safari suit. He spoke English with an Indian syllabicity, forming his words in the very front of his mouth, but he was fluent and quite at ease. "How may I help you?" he asked.

"Mr. Khan, I'm an American police officer, at present the guest of the Singapore authorities. They are allowing me to participate in their investigation of the Tan murders."

Khan nodded his head very slightly. "So Superintendent Lee has informed me."

"I know the value of your time, sir. May I ask a few questions?"

"Certainly."

"Obviously you have thousands of employees here of different backgrounds. Does this cause any language problems?"

Khan seemed slightly surprised at the question. "Yes, it does," he replied. "In fact it is a continuing one. Also our work schedules are complicated by many different religious holidays that have to be observed. There is hardly a day when the whole work force is available."

"Do you provide cafeteria facilities for your people?"

"Yes, and that involves another set of problems. I should not speak, I am a vegetarian, but with at least four major religious groups in our work force, we have to provide acceptable food for them all, without giving offense to anyone. Fortunately, our people understand this and we have it well worked out."

"Thank you. Do the secret societies cause any special difficulties?"

"Not ordinarily, because jobs here are valued and society members are careful not to lose them. They did try

196

something recently, but Engineer Tan, as you well know, reported it. Of course we already knew."

"How?" Tibbs asked.

"We have inspectors who work in the evening, checking what was done during the day. They discovered the dummy duct almost immediately. You see, Mr. Tibbs, that sort of thing is nothing new; it happens all the time. Usually we stop it, sometimes we let it go through. When we do that, we notify the authorities where the ship is going. You must read in the papers frequently that secret caches have been found on board ship by your Coast Guard. Then large amounts of drugs are seized—and taken off the market."

"When your inspectors discovered the false duct, was your chief of security told?"

"Of course. That is his job. It was through him that I was notified. Normally the matter would have been handled at a lower level, but because of the unhappy murders. . ."

"I understand," Tibbs said. "Mr. Khan, do you normally promote by seniority or ability?"

"Always by ability. It is much the better way."

"Does this generate hard feelings?"

Khan smiled and spread his hands. "Mr. Tibbs, our people are human—all of them. But if someone is promoted ahead of them, it encourages them to do a better job. Then, next time, they will be chosen. Our policy is known to all our employees."

"I have other questions," Tibbs said, "but I don't need to trouble you with them personally. Thank you for your time."

"A pleasure, Mr. Tibbs. Come and see me anytime you wish."

From the shipyard Tibbs went to the offices of the *Straits Times*, where he located a journalist familiar with the conditions in China in the northern regions. The man was quite willing to talk and did. Once again Tibbs took extensive notes and asked some very pointed questions. Satisfied with the result, he returned to the hotel where Miriam was waiting rather anxiously for him.

"I certainly know that you can take care of yourself," she said, "but not in your present condition. Tom Millbrae has invited us to dinner, upstairs. I accepted."

"All right."

"You don't sound very enthusiastic, but I can understand. I won't let it drag on."

"Bless you," Tibbs said, and went into his own room to lie down.

When the meal was over and all the proper things had been said, Virgil announced that he was going out again. "No, you're not!" Miriam protested, but this time he would not be deterred.

"I have one more thing to do," he said, "and it won't wait. This time it's nothing dangerous; I'm just going to pay a call."

"Would you like me to come with you?"

"Much as I would enjoy—"

"All right, I'll stay here. But please, Virgil, don't do anything rash."

"I wouldn't think of it," he said, and let himself out the door.

Ten minutes later the phone rang. When Miriam answered, it was Lee. "Let me talk to Virgil," he said.

"I can't, he's gone out again."

"At night? Where?"

"He didn't tell me. All he said was that he had one more thing to do; a call he had to pay."

"Nothing beyond that?"

"Only that it wouldn't be anything dangerous. Roger, he's hardly fit to be on his feet."

"I know that, Miriam. Right now I could kick him squarely in the butt. If he wanted to go somewhere he should have let me know." Lee hung up abruptly.

Inspector Cheng was somewhat surprised when a civilian taxi pulled up and Virgil Tibbs got out. The Khe Bong Neighborhood Police Post was quite close to the roadway, which made observation easy. Automatically Cheng straightened his coat and then waited for the man he knew was an American police detective, even though they had never met. He had seen a film about him and that was enough.

Tibbs came in and presented his card. Cheng introduced himself and then held open the half-door that gave access to the inside of the post. He led the way to the main inner room, poured a cup of coffee, and handed it to his guest. "Did you come to see our station?" he asked.

"Yes," Tibbs answered. "By any chance were you in command when the first of the Tan murders was discovered?"

"Yes, I was. It was a horrible sight. But you must have seen many like it."

Tibbs tried the coffee, which was two stages removed from battery acid, and made his request. "I'm not allowed to visit any crime scenes," he said, "because I can't be here to testify. But I wondered if I could see something of this housing project."

"Would you like a tour?"

"If possible."

"Then I'll be happy to take you myself. My sergeant can take over, and we have radio communications if I'm needed."

Cheng gave no indication that he was being imposed upon; rather he seemed to enjoy the idea that the American who had been talked about so much lately had chosen to come by. At the same time he noticed that his guest was favoring his left side as he walked. "Are you quite well?" he asked.

"I'm just fine, thank you."

Cheng thought otherwise, but let it pass. He led the way to the main tower of the Toa Payoh Housing Estate, which was only a few steps, summoned an elevator, and took Tibbs up to the top floor. "How much do you wish to see?" he asked.

"As much as you care to show me."

"This has reference to the Tan case, does it not?"

"Yes, it does. Superintendent Lee has given me the privilege of working on it with him."

It took almost an hour to complete the tour. Cheng supplied a great deal of information, in addition to which Tibbs asked a number of questions. When they reached the seventh floor, Cheng led the way down a corridor and then stopped. "This is the Tan apartment," he said. "I remember what you said about visiting any crime scenes, but all the evidence has been removed for some time. It is now unoccupied. Would you care to go inside?"

"If you're sure it will be all right."

For answer Cheng slipped a master key into the lock and opened the door.

Tibbs's first impression was how small it was. There was a tiny living area, a kitchen, a minimal bathroom, and two very limited bedrooms. How six people had managed to live there he did not know, even though four of them had been children. Obviously bunk beds had been the answer.

Having committed himself, Tibbs spent some time in the compact apartment. Then he carefully looked out the windows, checked how far they would open, and examined the lock on the door. Twenty minutes later he returned with his guide to the police post, to find Lee waiting for him there. "Don't you ever go home and rest?" he asked in a not-too-cordial tone.

"How did you—"

"I called you, but Miriam told me you'd gone out 'to pay a call.' Since you don't know anybody here well enough to drop in unannounced at their home, I did a little deducting. Then I phoned here, and bingo."

"Brilliant," Tibbs said.

"Elementary, my dear Tibbs. Now that you've put me to all this trouble, what have you learned?"

"The motive for the Tan killings," Virgil answered.

Chapter Twenty-Three

Lee drove him back to the Crossroads. They had gone several blocks in silence when Lee at last asked, "Virgil, do you remember what I asked you to do before you contacted any of our people?"

"Yes," Tibbs answered, "and for once in my cotton-picking life I plain forgot. I had something on my mind that pushed everything else aside. I plead guilty."

"I'm sure you understand," Lee said, "that everyone involved in any way with the Tan killings is pretty much on edge these days. That goes double at the Khe Bong Neighborhood Post. Fortunately Cheng is a good fellow and we get along well, so he'll cover for me."

"I don't understand."

"Arthur Sim's invitation to you to cooperate in the Tan investigation was principally to give you something to do while the final details of the Motamboru case are being sorted out. That doesn't mean that your help isn't appreciated; it definitely is. You're a top pro, and we know it. But we have to cover our own butts, because this is our baby and we're expected to rock it. So I promised the deputy commissioner that I'd have you clear any police contacts through me. To help you as much as to help us."

"I get the picture," Tibbs said.

"Good. You threw Cheng a curve: he didn't know you were coming, and he didn't know how much he was supposed to tell you. That put him on the spot. Officially, you did call me first and I cleared it with Cheng, if anyone asks. No one will, but please, don't do this to me again."

"You have my word," Tibbs promised.

There was nothing more said until Lee pulled up in front of the hotel. There they exchanged goodnights before Tibbs went inside and up to the suite. He spoke only briefly to Miriam before he sat down and buried himself in his own thoughts. Miriam was reading. She sensed his mood immediately and left him strictly alone, turning her pages quietly and staying where she was.

Finally Tibbs looked up. "I dropped the ball tonight," he said.

"We all do that occasionally," Miriam replied. "I remember something Mark Twain said. 'Everyone is entitled to make a damn fool of himself five minutes each day. Wisdom consists in not exceeding the limit.' "

"Thanks for those comforting words," Tibbs said. "Now I'm trying to think something out. I don't smoke: if I did, it would be a three-pipe problem."

Miriam looked at him. "I was raised on Sherlock Holmes. *The Red-Headed League,* as I recall."

"You're a pearl among women," Tibbs said.

"Yes, I know that. I want some hot chocolate; how about you?"

"Fine."

"I'll pour you three cups. Perhaps they will help."

At nine the following morning, they were having breakfast in the coffee shop, surrounded by tourists, when Lee appeared. He so far unbent as to kiss Miriam on the cheek before he sat down without waiting to be invited. He ordered coffee and then turned to Tibbs. "I'm sorry if I came down on you too hard last night," he said.

"You didn't," Tibbs answered. "You were dead right. Mea culpa."

"How did you sleep?"

"Mostly I didn't; I had some things to figure out."

"Any success?"

"I think so. After we eat, I want to pay a call. But only if you'll come with me."

"All right."

When they had finished, Miriam excused herself, leaving the two men alone. They went outside to Lee's car. "Where would you like to go?" Lee asked.

"To the shipyard," Tibbs said.

In response, Lee started the engine and drove out into traffic once more. "The key man there is Quek Jew Kiang, the head of security," he said.

"Once a policeman in the north of China before he came here," Virgil added.

"That's right; it's in the file. I admire your memory, Virgil: Chinese names are usually hard for Westerners. Are you planning to interview Tan?"

"I'm sure you've gotten all there is to get out of him," Virgil answered. "I'd rather not plague the man anymore."

"You've got me baffled, Virgil. What do you have in mind?"

"A tour of the shipyard, if that's possible—from the security angle."

"Of course it's possible." Lee wanted to ask more, but he made a deliberate decision not to press Virgil at that point. Instead he drove to the shipyard, parked the car, and took Tibbs inside to meet his friend Quek.

Although they were not expected, the security chief made them welcome in his small utilitarian office. "How can I help?" he asked.

Lee handled things very well. He explained that Tibbs was on a visit to the city, that he had cleared up the Motamboru matter, and that while he was waiting for final disposition of the case, he had been invited to join Lee ex officio.

Quek nodded his understanding. He ran his hands through his thinning hair and pushed some paper to one side on his desk. "I'll get Tan up here," he offered. "He's used to it by now."

"Excuse me," Virgil said, "but since Roger has already interviewed him several times, I doubt if I could get anything more out of him."

"I'm forced to agree," Quek said. "What would you like?"

"A tour of the shipyard. One that would take us to the area where Tan's design is being constructed. I understand you have an undercover man there."

Quek turned to Lee. "I presume you told him that."

"Yes, I did. He's cleared."

"That's all I need," Quek said. "Let's go. To make it look good, I'll have to take you around a bit."

"I'd like that," Tibbs said. "I've never seen a shipyard."

Quek handed over two hard hats and donned a third that had his name on it. "The color means security," he explained. "We can go anywhere with them on."

Quek led the way outside and then stopped for a moment. "How much time do you have?" he asked.

"As much as we need," Tibbs replied.

The security chief seemed to welcome that answer. He unplugged a golf cart and put his guests inside. Lee chose to sit in back and let Tibbs ride up front with Quek. The cart took off, and they began to roll down the long length of the massive shipyard.

"A shipyard is a very complicated operation," Quek explained. "Whether it's repair or new construction, hundreds of trades are involved. Plumbers, welders, carpenters, cabinetmakers, painters, locksmiths, steamfitters, riggers, crane operators—it goes on and on."

"How stable is the employment?" Tibbs asked.

"Quite stable. We usually have one or two jobs waiting to fill every dock or construction site we have."

"Your English is very good."

"It has to be; I also speak Mandarin, Cantonese, and three northern Chinese dialects."

"Were you at the university?"

Quek raised his voice to be heard over the din of a high noise area. "No, I just picked it up."

As he drove on, he explained what they were seeing. Twice he stopped the cart and took them on foot into a construction area. During all of this Lee remained silent, but paid close attention to what was going on. At times the three men had to squeeze past piles of materials and through narrow passageways. The pounding of riveters' hammers at one point reached ear-splitting intensity; then the hissing of steam hoses took over as the footing became difficult and tricky.

When they were free of that area, they stopped in front of the bow of a huge new ship that was nearing completion. "This is the job that Tan is on," Quek said. "I'll take you through it from the top down."

It was a very long climb that left all three men short of breath in the tropical heat. What at last they reached the open top deck, they were rewarded with a panoramic view of the shipyard and the seemingly limitless harbor. In the opposite direction lay the unique city of Singapore. Even Lee took time to drink in the spectacle.

Quek then led the way down through the intricate maze of the ship under construction. Some sections were all but completed; others were little more than framework and hazardous. Then Quek stopped, apparently to point something out. "It's just the other side of this bulkhead," he said. "Please don't show any unusual interest."

It would have been hard to do so; the construction area looked exactly like many others they had already seen, with

206

Chinese workmen in hard hats going about their work. Tibbs took just the right amount of time, giving apparently casual interest to the scene; then he went on through, following the others.

More than an hour later they returned to Quek's office where they sat down for a welcome rest. "Something cold to drink?" Quek suggested.

Virgil declined. "I'd like to ask a few questions," he said. "Roger, you know Madam Wee, Tan's wife. Is she an attractive woman?"

"No," Lee answered. "In talking with her husband I called her that out of courtesy, but actually she isn't."

"Do you think that Tan is happy with her? I know it was an arranged marriage."

"There's no doubt there, Virgil. She's a very good wife to him."

"Did you run across any rejected suitors—before she was married?"

"I doubt that she had any. The family came here from northern China when she was sixteen. Not being Straits born, and without any English, she was fortunate her parents found her such a good husband."

"She's not likely to be the object of someone's sexual desires, then."

"No. That was thoroughly checked out. Nothing there at all."

"I thought not," Tibbs said, "but I wanted to be sure."

"Please, I want to hear your ideas," Quek said.

Virgil waited for several seconds, as though he were forestalling the moment when he would have to declare himself. When he did begin to speak, it was almost as though it were a soliloquy.

"In my experience I've seen three kinds of murder. The first is specific, where some particular person is wanted dead: out of hatred, greed, revenge, or a whole hatful of

207

other motives. But they all come down to the same thing: the desire to kill one particular person, or group of persons."

Tibbs stopped, then locked his fingers together in a tight grip. "The second kind of murder has accidental victims: people in the wrong place at the wrong time. A sniper on a rooftop may kill anyone he can get in his sights without caring who they are. He may be in a demented frenzy, but that doesn't do anything to help his victims."

He looked at the other two men, who were waiting silently for him to continue. "The third kind of murder is symbolic. Someone becomes enraged at society and resolves to kill a policemen—any policeman will do. The fact that he represents law and order is enough. Or a teacher: any one of a group significant to the killer."

"The Tan killings can't be accidental or symbolic, as you put it," Quek said. "Not with three children attacked in one family. It has to be specific."

Slowly Tibbs shook his head. "I thought so too at first, but the evidence is all against it. The Tan family has been exhaustively investigated. Roger, you and your team kept at it until there were no more places to look, or any more questions to ask, and you came up empty. That's a strong indication they weren't specific victims.

"Envy is a powerful motive, but obviously it doesn't apply here. The Tan family lived in a small high-rise apartment. A very modest one with simple furniture. According to information in the library, seventy-eight percent of the people in Singapore have the same kind of housing. That's one of the first things I looked up.

"Tan has a good job, but a great many people in Singapore make much more than he does. By the way, what's being done about the dummy duct the secret society was trying to get him to add to the ship?"

"We had a meeting on that with our management and

the police," Quek answered. "It was decided to have him go ahead and design it in. It can be removed later. In strictest confidence, we want to catch the criminals red-handed."

"Tan is cooperating?"

"Yes, completely. Also he's keeping his mouth shut, pretending that he's doing it for the money and out of fear of the society."

"I've never been to China," Tibbs said. "I understand a lot has been accomplished by the communists, but at a high price in human terms."

"That's true," Quek agreed. "The people are very regimented; often they can't choose their own professions. They have to do whatever they're told."

"Did you choose to become a policeman?"

"No, I was assigned. That's one reason I wanted to get out—and did."

"With your wife?"

"No. She's a dedicated party member. Everything was politics to her. When she refused to come with me, I didn't care."

"Did you have any other family?"

"My sister. I wanted her very much to come, but she is married and her husband refused to let her."

That seemed to satisfy Tibbs for the moment. Lee shuffled his feet a little, then thought better of it. All this had to have a point, but as yet he failed to see what it was.

"I know that every fourth person in the world is Chinese," Virgil continued. "and that China has a severe overpopulation problem. At present only one child is allowed per family. Exceptions are made for twins, of course, or if the first child is deformed or deficient in some way."

"That's right," Lee said, "but why—" Then, abruptly he closed his mouth.

"I saw a film on American television," Tibbs went on.

"It had to do with rural life in modern China. In one sequence there was a married woman who was pregnant for the second time. She was mercilessly hounded to have an abortion. Finally, when her baby was more than six months along, she was compelled to consent. The film showed her having a massive injection through her abdomen, one that would kill the child in her womb."

Lee stared at Tibbs. Then he silently closed his hands into fists, keeping a tight rein on himself.

"I assume the Chinese police won't cooperate in an investigation like this, but, by any chance, did that also happen to your sister?"

"Why are you asking me?" Quek demanded.

Tibbs's voice was very calm and unemotional. "The person responsible for the Tan murders had to be someone who had fairly close contact with the family. The phone calls proved that that person knew exactly how many children there were. There was no secret to that, of course, but it was significant.

"All of the neighbors in the high rise were exhaustively questioned, with no result. I read all of the interviews in the file. Most of the families had children or were expecting them. The Tans had few outside activities. Tan himself belongs to no clubs or societies. That left his employment, by a process of elimination, as the remaining place to look."

Lee got up and stood by the window.

"It's obvious from what you told me that your wife refused to have even the one child that is now allowed. You're very close to your sister; you showed that when you asked her to leave China with you, even though she had a husband."

"She already has a child, a daughter," Quek said.

"Yet despite that you still tried to get her to come with you. You see, Mr. Quek, it's been widely publicized that two of the Tan children were killed, but nothing whatever was let out that a third child had been attacked. Fortunately the child is recovering, but a little while ago you referred to three of the Tan children having been victims.

"The whole business of the fake conduit brought Engineer Tan very much to your attention. As security chief you had access to every available detail about him, including the size of his family. He had had four children in six years, with the possibility of more. You were denied children by a militant wife more interested in politics than in having even the allowed small family.

"Your sister's one child is a daughter, not a son so important in Chinese society. If your sister were also forced to have an abortion, at a time when her pregnancy was well along . . ."

Quek sat frozen for a few moments, then his face began to betray his intense inner emotions. "Are you suggesting that because my sister—" he began, but he could not continue. The inner burning, suppressed rage that had tormented him for so long took possession of him and overflowed into words. His voice shook as he told the horrible truth. "They killed her and her son *three weeks* before he would have been born."

"Madam Wee also comes from northern China," Tibbs said.

Quek's voice became icy cold. "It was a leader of the Wee family who demanded the abortion. Her husband wrote me that, after they had murdered her."

Lee moved quietly forward. "Let us go downtown together," he said in Mandarin. "I will help you."

"I would like to be alone for a short while," Quek replied. "You are my friend. Allow me his."

"You have a gun in your desk?"

"Yes."

"I'm sorry," Lee said. "I can't allow that."

"Understand that it had to be done," Quek said, still in

Mandarin. "A Wee took my sister's life, and her son's, while another Wee was producing babies one after another. There had to be justice."

For a moment the two men, who had been friends, looked at each other. Then, silently, Lee reached for his handcuffs. For a moment he thought Quek was going to try something desperate, and he was ready, but Quek stood up and put his hands behind his back with quiet acceptance. "The court will understand," he said.

For the first time, Lee showed the massive emotion that had been building up within him. "I don't think so," he answered.

Chapter Twenty-Four

When he got back to the suite at the Crossroads, Virgil was grateful to find that Miriam was not there. He was in no mood to see or talk to anyone, and he had no appetite whatever for lunch. He shed his coat, kicked off his shoes, and stretched on his back across his bed. He folded his hands behind his head and stared up at the ceiling.

With a deliberate effort he calmed his breath, closed his eyes, and tried to immerse his mind in thoughts of calm infinity. It had worked for him many times in the past, and he wanted desperately for it to work for him now. But like a recording angel giving testimony before the Sublime Court, to which only God appoints the judges, the pages of the Tan file were paraded past him one by one. The case was over, but it would not go away.

He wanted very much to go home, to take up the routine of the life he had chosen, but thoughts about Miriam refused to be excluded. Her husband had only been dead a few months. He had been a head of state: a man of world stature and importance. Miriam came from a wealthy home and had an education well beyond his own, even though he had a university degree magna cum laude.

At her level, questions of heritage did not arise. He knew a baseball player who was also black, had little education, and suffered from his appearance. But he could throw strikes and get big-league hitters out, one after another. His team didn't care how he looked, as long as his arm held up.

In contrast Miriam had it all. Her appearance was just part of the package. She would certainly want to leave Singapore soon, but he had no idea where she would go. Perhaps back to Switzerland, where her children were in school. Returning to Bakara would be much too dangerous, and her future there was very much in doubt. She possibly could become another Indira Ghandi, but if so she would constantly face the same tragic fate.

She could have asylum in the United States for the asking, but she might not want it. She was more European in her outlook.

He knew he had been skirting the issue, and that it was time to face facts. When he had posed as her husband, he had been forced to keep himself rigidly in line. The fact that she was an utterly desirable woman had had to be ignored. Now they were very much together, without her children this time, and sharing a hotel suite. Under these altered circumstances his feelings toward her had grown to the point where he knew that no matter what happened, no other woman would ever be able to take her place in his life.

But there was a cold fact he had to face: normally her world was one of elegant society, diplomacy, and affairs of state. Other than as a friend, she was far out of his reach. In no way was she cut out to be the wife of a working policeman.

At that moment in his thoughts the door to the suite opened and Miriam came in. He did not know how she sensed he was there, but almost at once she came through the open doorway into his room. "Are you all right?" she asked.

"Yes," he answered.

He heard her shoes fall onto the floor, then the bed moved as she lay down beside him. "Tell me about it," she invited.

He turned toward her and looked at her lovely and compassionate face. She was just far enough away to keep from making it a physical thing. What she was offering was friendship of a rare and special kind.

He kept his voice calm and factual. "The Tan case is over. The two remaining children in the family are safe. Lee made the arrest, and I'm pretty sure I won't have to testify."

"Would you like to tell me about it?"

"I'd rather not."

"Then I'll read about it in the papers." She hesitated. "What are you going to do now?"

He reached an arm toward her. "Do you object to being kissed?" he asked.

"Not by you."

He kissed her warmly and held her next to him for a few moments. Then he forced himself to get up.

"Now that I know where you are, I have something to do," he said, and went to the telephone.

He spoke first with Henderson Chang, the manager of the Crossroads. "Could you be free at two-thirty this afternoon?" he asked.

"Certainly."

"And can I come down for a brief conference in a few minutes?"

"By all means."

That done, he called the embassy and found the ambassador in. "Mr. Thatcher," he said, "Mrs. Motamboru would appreciate seeing you this afternoon on an important matter."

"I understand," Thatcher said.

"For reasons of security, I suggest that we meet here at the hotel. Would two-thirty be convenient?"

"I'll make it," Thatcher said.

"Thank you, sir. In Mr. Chang's office."

"Good." The ambassador hung up.

Next Virgil called Lee, who was in his office doing the inevitable paperwork that went with any arrest. "Roger, there'll be a meeting here this afternoon at two-thirty. I believe you'll want to attend."

"Sorry, Virgil, but I can't. Not a chance."

"Let me put it this way: I think it's important that you accept."

"If that's how it is, I'll make it."

"Henderson Chang's office."

"Good thinking. He often serves Sacher torte, and that's my weakness."

"Ten to one he knows it."

"No bet. See you then."

All that accomplished, Virgil went down and spent a few minutes with Henderson Chang. During the interview, he was careful to mention that Assistant Superintendent Lee would be attending the meeting at two-thirty. Chang had smiled. "I'll be ready for him," he promised.

As soon as Virgil got back to the suite, the phone rang. Arthur Sim's secretary was on the line. "The deputy commissioner's compliments," she said. "He would like to know if Madam Motamboru and you could join him and some other officers for a social dinner this evening."

"We'd be delighted," Tibbs responded.

"Thank you, sir. A car will call for you at seven."

Due largely to the professionalism of everyone concerned, the meeting in Henderson Chang's office convened exactly at the time scheduled. Almost immediately the refreshment cart was wheeled in. Miriam accepted a cup of tea. Lee was handed a slice of Sacher torte without his asking. Tibbs declined to have anything. Ambassador Thatcher was relaxed and comfortable, as though he had already anticipated everything that would be said. He accepted coffee, tasted it, and smiled his approval.

"Since Mr. Tibbs set up this meeting," Chang said, "I defer to him."

Virgil began quietly. "As you all know, President Motamboru of Bakara was a close personal friend of our President. The two men saw eye-to-eye on a great many issues. During the last months of his life, Mr. Motamboru carefully documented the efforts of the communist powers to force their way into Africa. Bakara, being a democracy, was a particular target. The tactics used, the size of the forces, the identity of key individuals, and their known objectives, were all carefully detailed. He offered to supply a copy of his dossier to our President, knowing that it would be of great value to the United States.

"When Mrs. Motamboru left Bakara, she brought this file with her, intending to hand it personally to the American ambassador in Switzerland. Instead she was intercepted and diverted here. As soon as she arrived, she made a private appointment with Mr. Chang. She assumed correctly that the man in charge of a hotel of this stature, where world figures are regularly accommodated, would be totally reliable and discreet.

"She told Mr. Chang she was carrying something that had to be especially safeguarded. Mr. Chang accepted the package, left his office, and returned in a few minutes with a key to a vault drawer. When this drawer was later officially opened, it was found to be empty. Obviously Mr. Chang had taken special precautions."

The hotel manager maintained his total composure. "Do I have a problem with the police?" he asked.

"I doubt it," Lee responded. "If your vault had been robbed, we would have known it within minutes. Or if any hotel personnel had made a disastrous mistake."

"It seems to me," the ambassador said, "that Mr. Chang was given an extraordinary trust and that he proved worthy of it. If that package had been found when the box was opened, it would have been read by unauthorized people. Honorable, no doubt, but with no authority to see such sensitive material."

"Let me suggest that we settle this matter, if possible," Chang said. "Madam, do you now wish to have your property returned to you?"

"Yes," Miriam answered.

In response Chang unlocked a drawer in his desk, took out a small package, and handed it to her. "Is that the same one?" he asked.

"It is. Thank you, sir."

"For your information," Chang added, "I took the package in question from where it was being kept a few minutes ago. My office has been under continuous guard since then."

Miriam turned to Thatcher. "My husband instructed me to see that this package reached your President personally. Can you arrange that?"

"Yes, Mrs. Motamboru. As soon as I return to the embassy, I'll call and tell him that it's on the way. It will go by diplomatic pouch, specifically marked for the President's eyes only."

"There's a police escort waiting for you outside," Lee said. "Four of our motorcycle officers will see you to the embassy. I set it up, just in case."

The meeting broke up quickly after that.

Chapter Twenty-Five

For the dinner to which she and Virgil had been invited, Miriam had chosen a simple rose silk dress that was exactly right for the occasion. She looked stunning as she sat comfortably in the back of the executive police car that was taking them smoothly through the streets of Singapore. It passed several of the distinctive high rises made to look like three gigantic cubes piled atop one another, and through sections of old buildings that dated back to another, all-but-forgotten era. After some time the car pulled up in front of what appeared to be a small hotel.

Inside the modest lobby Sim was waiting to greet them. From the moment they came in, he was the ideal host. He led the way into a private dining room, where a number of others were waiting. A glance at the table told Tibbs that the food was to be Western. A Chinese meal would have called for round tables with places for ten; the one set up was rectangular and prepared to seat fourteen.

With amiable sociability the deputy commissioner introduced members of his staff. Among them were Osman Bin Mohamed, the commander of the Prosecutions Division, Pandian Subramaniam, Dalip Singh, Roger Lee, Superintendent Jurong of the Intelligence Division, and Ajit Singh, who had met Tibbs on his arrival. Miriam was the only woman present.

As soon as the introductions had been performed, two waiters scurried in to take orders for drinks. A small group of men gathered around Miriam, who took less than three minutes to have them all captivated. When Sim carefully steered her to a second group of guests, she joined them easily and, without apparent effort, acknowledged each of them by name, a sure key to popularity.

There was talk of the day's events at the Singapore Turf Club, the only legal betting facility in the country. Tactfully, no one asked Miriam concerning any of the special sights that Singapore had to offer, since she had had little opportunity to visit any of them.

When dinner was ready, Sim put Miriam at his right, Tibbs at his left. Although the facility did not appear pretentious, the food was superb and the service flawless. Tibbs was asked many things about his police work, as well as his opinion of some films based on his career. "I prefer the first one," he said, because there was no polite way he could decline. "It was about a real case that came my way. The others were fiction."

Despite this polite conversation, Miriam was clearly the center of attention. For the first time he saw her in her element. Without in any way putting herself forward, she kept the conversation moving, answered questions about her country and her life, and, to Virgil's embarrassment, told how he had rescued her from kidnappers. By the time the dessert was served, every man present had become her loyal admirer.

When the coffee had been poured, Arthur Sim informally took the floor. "I am a great believer in the international police fraternity," he said. "None of us took up the work we do with the expectation that it would make us rich or famous." He produced a package from under the table and from it took a framed certificate. "Virgil, I'd like you to accept this with our gratitude. It makes you officially an honorary member of the Singapore Police. And here is one of our uniform hats for you to add to your collection."

Virgil accepted the gifts with a tightness in his throat. "I'm very honored, sir," he said. "And proud to be part of such an admirable organization. Thank you."

"Now, perhaps," Sim continued, "you will be kind enough to show us how you arrived at the conclusion you did in the Tan case. At our first meeting, you told me that you could almost guarantee that a foreigner, specifically a Caucasian, wasn't responsible. Suppose you start there."

Virgil knew there was no way out. "First of all, sir, I considered the size of the buildings where the crimes occurred. It clearly houses hundreds of people, and probably has some turnover. This means that no normal person could possibly know them all, or tell by sight who belongs in the building and who does not. I had already been told that almost all of the residents were Chinese. Also that nothing that happens in a predominantly Chinese area goes unnoticed. I concluded that a Chinese could almost certainly go in and out without being detected as a nonresident, but for a Caucasian, it would be virtually impossible."

"How did Quek get into the apartment?"

"One of two ways. As chief of security he would probably have lock picks; many policemen carry them for emergency use. They're simple to use, and the locks in the housing project, I noticed, are quite ordinary.

"While taking us on a tour, he listed some of the trades needed at the shipyard. One of them was locksmiths. It's hot there, and almost no one keeps his coat on. Quek was in contact with Tan because of the dummy duct business. He could have lifted Tan's keys from his coat and had copies made. Ordinary key duplication is routine and isn't questioned."

"Those are interesting details," Sim said, "but now I'm concerned to know why he chose the Tan family for his victims. Also what caused you to suspect him in the first place."

"It was a process of elimination, sir, based on the exhaustive work your people had already done," Tibbs answered. "When I was given a copy of the case file, I studied it carefully. It showed that most of the usual motives could be eliminated. Madam Wee is a good and faithful wife, not likely to attract any outside admirers. Tan himself checked out in every way as an ideal husband and father. There was no hint of any sexual motivation, any use of narcotics, criminal involvement, or family conflicts. Tan earns a good salary and visibly lives within it. There's no hint at all that he ever kept a mistress or involved himself with other women.

"Very clearly the attacks on those children, three out of four, were not random, the work of a murderous pedophile searching for any victim he could get, of either sex. Therefore the motive had to lie much deeper. And as you know, sir, motives like that can result in the most violent and horrible acts."

Sim nodded his agreement, but did not interrupt.

"The only irregularity of any kind in Tan's life seemed to be his involvement in the dummy duct business. He had reported it, opening the possibility that a terrible revenge was being taken. But he had reported it in secret, and the secret had been kept. Otherwise Quek could never have placed an undercover man in the work crew and gotten away with it, as he did.

"I know almost nothing about shipbuilding except that it is a very complicated business. But even simple manufacturing processes include inspectors who check the work being done; there are hundreds of inspectors in automobile assembly plants. I therefore assumed that there had to be inspectors at the shipyard and unless they too were part of the conspiracy, the dummy duct would have been discovered.

"Superintendent Lee wrote a very clear and full report on his conversation with Quek concerning the duct and the secret society concerned. At that time Quek put it all on the basis of Engineer Tan's report. He was talking in confidence with a responsible police officer whom he knew, but he never mentioned any previous knowledge of the irregularity.

"That set me thinking because if the inspectors had found the duct, the chief of security would be one of the first to be notified. To settle the point I called on the managing director of the shipyard. When I mentioned the duct, he told me flat out that the inspectors had detected it well before Tan came forward. Obviously Quek had not been candid with Lee, and I wanted to know why.

"Now, sir, suppose you were in Quek's position and you had just been told that an engineer in the plant had been making an unauthorized design. What would you do?"

"I'd start checking on the engineer immediately."

"Undoubtedly that's exactly what Quek did. His first step would be to pull Tan's personnel file. Now something that I found very different in Singapore: married women still go by their maiden names. There's a copy of Tan's file in the docket I was given; his wife's name is given as Wee Lai Chan and her birthplace the same general region of northern China from which Quek came. Staring him in the face on the same piece of paper was the fact that the Tans had had four children in six years.

"I don't need to tell you, sir, how strong family ties are in China. I happened to have seen a film about forced abortion in China. Quek had built up a terrible hatred against the Wee family, because a Wee had forced his sister to have an abortion when her son was close to being delivered. It cost her her life. Quek's wife is an ardent party member who refused to bear him a child, hopefully a son, or to come with him when he left China. He did very much love his sister, and when she was robbed of *her* son, and her life, by the Wees, his hatred exploded. He concealed what he knew about Tan and the duct in order to extract his vengeance against them."

"But they were innocent," Ajit Singh pointed out.

"Of course they were, but that made no difference. In the United States we have had recent cases where fanatical persons of Armenian descent have attacked innocent people of Turkish extraction to avenge a massacre that took place in 1915.

"As to the crime itself, Quek would have had no trouble entering the housing complex well after midnight and, at that hour, opening the door of the Tan apartment and slipping inside. The child was killed in a manner that prevented her from crying out. The murder was not discovered immediately, which left Quek enough time to disappear."

"Have you any thoughts on the other two attacks?" Sim asked.

"When Quek confesses, and he will, those questions will be answered. The boy was old enough to know where his father worked. He was probably picked up on his way home from school. If Quek had approached him by name, driving a shipyard car, the boy would probably have trusted him."

"He could have used any number of excuses," Subramaniam observed, "and the shipyard cars are plainly marked."

"How the little girl was poisoned is harder," Tibbs continued. "I know of a case where a vendor giving out samples of a soft drink put LSD in some of the cups. Also PCP was baked in some cookies that were passed out at a retirement home in Los Angeles. Unfortunately, people never question such gift items. Even a child cautioned to stay away from strangers would see no reason why she couldn't accept a free cup of soft drink or a cookie."

When he had finished speaking, Virgil knew that as of that moment his work in Singapore was over. The sooner he left for home, the better. He would have liked to spend a day or two sightseeing, but his lavish suite was being paid for by the government, as well as his other expenses. He had no intention of overstaying his welcome.

There was no need to tell Arthur Sim of his decision; he was attending what was all too clearly a farewell dinner.

At the appropriate moment he looked at Miriam, who gave him a slight nod of her head. She spoke their thanks, he shook hands all around, and together they left in the car that had been patiently waiting for them.

When they were back in the suite, Virgil turned to her. "I want to tell you," he said, "that you were superb this evening. I was in awe of you."

Miriam sat down. "That was the kind of thing I'm used to, Virgil, although I won't be doing much of it anymore. I still have a few friends, but my position is different now. I'm sure you understand."

Virgil sat beside her. "Has it occurred to you," he asked, "that people will want to see you, and be with you, just for yourself?"

Miriam smiled and laid a hand on his. "Protocol doesn't work that way, Virgil. It never has. It's who you are, not who you were. It's all done with a purpose. Actually the constant maneuvering, the political gains or losses, are all part of the continuing struggle for power. It's been going on since Alexander the Great. If you want to know the truth, I'm glad to be out of it. Tell me, Virgil, what are you going to do now?"

"Go home." He said it very simply.

"To your work in Pasadena?"

"It's my job."

"You're a very talented man, Virgil. You could do many things."

He was touched by that. "I'd like to think so, Miriam, but you know how the headhunters work. It's not, 'Can you do the job?' but 'Have you done it before, recently?' I'm past the age of being a trainee in an entry-level position."

"You could set up your own agency."

"A friend of mine, Jack Tallon, left the Pasadena department to become chief of police in Whitewater, Washington. He's pretty happy there."

"Would a job like that suit you, Virgil?"

"I don't know; I haven't thought about it. What are your plans?"

"This last year has taken so much out of me, I haven't been able to think things out either. My husband is dead and has been for some time. If he were here, he would tell me to start building a new life for myself. I know it's what I should do, for me and for my children."

"I completely agree," Tibbs said. "You've got so much ahead of you."

Miriam squeezed his hand, thanking him for his support. "I know a very good job I'd like to have if I can get it."

"You don't need a job."

"Virgil, I can't just vegetate!" She sat a little straighter, crossed her legs, and clasped her hands around one knee. "When you first come to pose as my husband, back in Pasadena, I told you that I was a very good cook—remember?"

"I certainly do," he acknowledged. "You're a fabulous cook. But don't tell me you're planning on starting a restaurant."

226

"Oh, no, Virgil. I'm afraid I wouldn't be very good at that. But I do have some other assets."

"You speak several languages."

"Yes, that helps at times. Also I'm an efficient house-keeper. And I manage quite well on the social scene."

"At that you're fabulous—I just told you so."

She took a moment to rub the back of her neck. "Virgil, I've been through a great deal. I've been in a privileged position, but it's also brought some very bad times. I haven't been living on a bed of roses. Do you understand?"

"Yes," he answered.

"There are many individuals, Virgil, who can't stand seeing a woman like me better off than they think I should be. Especially among the so-called beautiful people. Whoever named them that was wrong. The really beautiful people are the ones who don't have a lot, but are always willing to share. If someone is in trouble, they offer to help. They donate blood to the Red Cross."

"You'd be surprised how much they help the police," Virgil added.

Miriam swallowed, composed herself, and looked at him, face to face. "I'm not a brand-new, untouched girl right out of the Swiss academy I attended. But I have a lot to give to a man able to help me forget all that I've been through. Someone, Virgil, like you."

For all his perception, that caught him unawares. He drew her to him and held her in his arms, gently and compassionately. His heart was pounding in a way he could not control.

When she spoke again, her head was turned to one side, against his chest. "Virgil, this isn't just a reaction after what's happened to me here. Please believe that."

"I do," he told her.

"I think with your help I could put everything behind me, all my unwanted memories, just to be with you. And

227

my children adore you. So tell me, Virgil, is the job open?"

"It's been waiting for you for a long time," he answered.

Miriam laid a hand on his cheek. "Do you believe at all in karma?" she asked.

"I'm beginning to," he admitted. "It explains so many things."

"Yes, it does. I think it was karma that we met when we did, so that you would come to me when I needed you."

Miriam brushed her hair back from in front of her face. "I've dreamed for years that I might someday have a peaceful, happy life, far away from the turmoil of international politics. My husband and I knew what might happen at home. He told me to make contingency plans. So I bought the house in Pasadena. Because it was such a nice one, and I was very happy when I lived there."

For many weeks and months, Virgil had wondered if he would ever see or hear from Miriam Motamboru again. Now he was in an elegant hotel suite in exotic Singapore, and she was here beside him.

"When we were together in Pasadena," he said, "I had strict instructions, because I was in a position of high trust. Plus which you were married, and way out of my reach in any event. But I couldn't help how I came to feel about you."

Miriam looked at him, her eyes telling him she wanted to hear what he was saying.

"Very simply," he continued, "you haven't been out of my mind one day since then. I did dare to hope that some day you might write . . ."

He stopped and took fresh hold of himself, before his emotions could run away with his self possession. "Miriam," he said, "I'm a working policeman who's more in love with you than you can imagine. That's all I have to offer."

She reached and kissed him. "That's far more than

enough," she said. "Virgil, there's a very powerful cure for what is afflicting both of us. It's closeness to someone who truly cares about you. Go put the DO NOT DISTURB sign on the door."

He waited for a moment, trying to control all the rampaging thoughts that were gyrating in his brain. Then he went and did the simple thing she had suggested. She was alone now, and he was free to think the once impossible thought: that she might become his life's partner—his wife.

He went back to her with his soul on fire. Miriam again put her hands on his shoulders, giving him herself and her trust. "Virgil, if you want it that way, we can belong to each other. Right now I want to be close to you. I want to live in your world, not mine. I can't imagine anything that would make me so happy."

"I think we should celebrate," Tibbs said.

"So do I. And if I'm going to live in America and be an American girl, I must learn to speak like one. Let me try, Virgil dear: shall we make it your place, or mine?"